#whereskayla

Quineka Ragsdale

This book is dedicated to our missing. You are not forgotten.

CONTENTS

Special thanks to Shayla Gardner and Brian Pearson

1 GARVEY MORNING NEWS

Garvey police are searching for 17-year-old Kayla Carlisle who disappeared from school Monday after lunch. Friends and classmates are reportedly unaware of what happened. Detectives currently have no leads in the whereabouts of Carlisle.

"I don't think Garvey PD is making my little girl's disappearance a priority, and the school needs to cooperate more," said Carlisle's mom, Ms. Washington.

Harriet Tubman High School has no surveillance cameras, and so far, no one has claimed to have seen Carlisle leave. Witnesses state that the last time they saw Carlisle was after an altercation she had with her boyfriend during lunch on Monday. Although many students who were questioned alleged Carlisle's boyfriend may have been abusive, he has an alibi as he returned to class after lunch when Carlisle was last seen. All Harriet Tubman High school students returned to class after the altercation.

Cheerleader captain, Kayla Carlisle has often been referred to as a local celebrity with more than 20,000 Instagram followers. Social media has brought attention to the disappearance of Carlisle, with the hashtag,

1

#whereskayla. Students throughout the city are using Carlisle's last post from Monday morning as a memorial of sorts. These posts often speculate Carlisle's whereabouts or offer friendly well wishes. Often dressed in short skirts and six-inch stiletto high heels, police believe she is simply being a teenager and expressing her freedom. Carlisle turned seventeen last Wednesday.

Retracing her steps from the last week, Carlisle was the guest of honor at an unsupervised teenage party last Saturday to celebrate her birthday. The party is said to have been attended by hundreds of students across the city. Although at times the party may have gotten rowdy and rambunctious, students say, nothing happened out of the ordinary.

A thorough search has been completed within Harriet Tubman High School and around Carlisle's neighborhood. Police said that they are following the case as they would with any missing person's report, but with no suspicion of foul play, the disappearance is questionable. "We're following this case just like we would any other," assured Detective Madison.

Carlisle is approximately five feet five inches tall and around 125 pounds with dark brown hair and brown eyes. If you have any information on the whereabouts of Kayla Carlisle, contact the Garvey police.

2 DETECTIVE MADISON

Bothered by the amount of coverage the Kayla Carlisle story was getting, Detective Madison declined to answer any more questions from the press. He didn't even want to take any more calls from people who supposedly had tips into Kayla's disappearance.

"Are you offering money for information?" one caller questioned. "I think the boyfriend did it," another caller hissed. Did what? he quickly thought to himself. The girl is missing, not dead.

He and his partner, Detective Johnson, were the lead detectives on the case and felt that the story was nothing more than a waste of their time. There was no suspicion of foul play for the teen. If it wasn't for social media, it wouldn't even be a case. He sat in his office trying to figure out how he could focus on a more pressing case. Since the Garvey Morning News story ran that morning, Ms. Washington had posted his name and phone number to Kayla's social media pages. He received so many desk calls that he had to find an intermediary. Seeing how frustrated he was, his chief encouraged Secretary Davis to answer his calls.

Rubbing his temples, Detective Madison closed his eyes for a second wishing he was on a vacation. Not that he knew what a vacation was. He hadn't been outside of the city in five years.

"Let's go, partner!" Detective Johnson broke his thoughts. He knew that meant his witness was ready for questioning. He followed Detective Johnson to the secluded room near the back of the precinct.

A scrawny teen slouched in the folded chair behind the rectangular table. Her tawny hair was fading. She didn't even flinch at the sound of the door opening. Her arms and sullen face appeared in need of a home-cooked meal. She started to fidget through an oversized bag that looked too expensive for a girl of her appearance.

"Thank you for joining us today, Jenna."

She pulled out a bejeweled cell phone decorated with ears. "Anything I can do to help," she murmured. She didn't even look at the detectives. Her eyes were glued to her cell phone, while she continuously flicked her index finger up the screen. Detective Madison figured she must have been on her social media page.

"I promise that this won't take long," Detective Johnson assured her. "Could you put your phone away while you tell us about the last time you saw Kayla?" Detective Johnson took his seat closest to the wall. Detective Madison followed by taking the seat next to him.

Jenna stopped scrolling. She emptied her lungs in an exasperated sigh, then dropped the sparkly ears into the purse. She sniffled before finally facing the detectives. Her eyes were bloodshot red with dark circles lingering beneath them. She dusted loose hair strands away from her face and placed them behind her ear, then leaned back into her seat.

"I know that this may be hard for you, but any information that you can give us will help a great deal. Now, you say that you and Kayla were best friends?" Detective Madison questioned.

"Yes. I mean, I knew her as good as anyone else. I haven't been here long, but she befriended me so fast. I felt like we were kindred spirits. No one liked me, but Kayla made sure that I always had somewhere to sit during lunch and at the games. She made sure that I was invited to all of the parties. She's a really nice girl."

"When was the last time that you saw her?" asked Detective Madison. He felt like the questioning was pointless, but hoped it didn't show.

"I was there when Brian started the fight with her at lunch."

"Brian's her boyfriend, right?" interjected Detective Johnson. Jenna nodded. Detective Johnson scribbled something onto his notepad.

Jenna gnawed on what was left of her fingernails as she nodded, then continued.

"Brian and Tiffany had something going on. I think everyone knew that except Kayla. It's sad that she had to find out like that, though."

"Find out what? Like what?" Detective Johnson asked. Detective Madison thought Detective Johnson was being too thorough. It was hard to get any truth out of teenagers, and this gossip was so typical of high school girls.

"Her birthday party, Saturday. Brian and Tiffany were getting it on right there. Kayla walked right in on them."

Detective Johnson nodded as he returned to his scribbling.

"Is this what started the fight?" Detective Madison asked in an attempt to sound caring. He leaned back into his seat. No need to pretend that he was taking notes. He didn't even bring a notepad with him.

"Yes. I was at the table eating lunch with Kayla. I tried to get her to ignore Brian because she was really hurt, but he walked right over to sell her those same lies. He grabbed her so hard that she started crying. The bell rang, and it was time to go back to class. I asked Kayla if she was okay for me to go, and she said she was going to stay to talk to Brian. I don't know why she kept giving him a chance."

"What do you think happened to her after that?" Detective Johnson inquired.

"I think she just ran away."

"Really?" Detective Madison sat back up into his seat, his attention now on Jenna.

"She was with Brian a really long time. She even lost her virginity to him. Her and Tiffany had been friends since middle school. I think she just needed to get away from them all."

"But, why would she leave without a trace?" Detective Johnson asked.

"That's what has me nervous. She texted me Monday and said she just needed some time to herself, but she hasn't said anything else since. Her mom is the one who has everyone freaking out."

Detective Madison couldn't agree more. Ms. Washington was so adamant about finding Kayla that her antics could be what was sabotaging the case.

"Can we see the text?" Detective Madison asked.

Jenna reached into her purse for the shiny ears. She scrolled and tapped until she found what she was looking for.

"Here." She shoved her phone into Detective Madison's face.

There was one text time stamped at 2:00 pm Monday.

The top of the screen read: *Kayla.*

Detective Madison read the text feed:

> *Where are you? Did you skip?*

> *Yes. I just needed to get away. I'll call you later.*

It was enough evidence for him. He passed the phone to Detective Johnson, who was already peering over his shoulder. Detective Johnson examined the phone for a few moments before finally passing it back to Jenna.

"Did she skip often?" Detective Johnson asked.

"No. I don't think so, but these are special circumstances. She was made the laughing stock of the school. I'd want to save face too." Jenna sat up straight in her chair, then slid her purse into her lap. "Her mom is making such a fuss that it's starting to make me nervous. I hope she texts me soon. If she does, I'll make sure to let you know."

Detective Madison stood while sliding his business card out of his pocket. He extended the card to Jenna.

"Thank you for coming in today." Jenna stood then slid the card into her purse. *This girl can't have been much taller than my twelve-year-old,* Detective Madison thought to himself.

Detective Johnson opened the door for her.

"I'm sure she'll turn up soon," he whispered to Jenna.

Jenna offered a faint smile. "I think so too." Detective Johnson walked with Jenna to the exit.

Detective Madison returned to his desk to find a new stack of messages. He shook his head. Sifting through the little pink sheets, Detective Madison tried to perform his due diligence.

She probably left the country. It's cheaper to get implants that way.

I think the boyfriend had her killed and is just using school as his alibi. Just like OJ.

Tiffany is a snake and wanted Brian all to herself.

Rumors, rumors, rumors. No clues. Detective Madison didn't bother reading anymore. He dropped the stack into the trash.

"More hearsay?" Detective Johnson returned.

"Everyone has a damn conspiracy theory. No facts. I'm not sure if these kids are trying to make our job harder on purpose, or if they think it's a funny joke," Detective Madison steamed.

"Quite a few students saw the disagreement between her and the boyfriend, but no one saw her leave. A thorough search was done in the school. I'm starting to think, like you, that she did just run away."

"I just hope she shows up today, so we can put this behind us."

"I was looking at her Instagram page earlier. Did you know that girl has more than 20,000 followers?"

"I looked at quite a few pictures on her page. It's part of the reason that I'm sure this is a runaway."

"She was very popular and a model student of Harriet Tubman High. Even my niece is a fan of that girl."

"A fan? Of a local high school kid?" Detective Madison was in disbelief.

"I know. I thought the same thing, but you know how these kids are, and something just doesn't sit right with me about that Jenna girl."

"She's a teenager. Sometimes, I feel like we don't even speak their language."

"Yea. You're probably right," Detective Johnson agreed.

Detective Madison's cell phone screamed. He took the phone from his hip to glance at the caller ID. *Shit.* He suddenly remembered that he promised his wife he'd pick up something for dinner. It took a split second before he determined it was best he answered the call instead of ignoring it. He was walking on eggshells because his wife had been threatening a divorce for months. His workload curtailed his time at home.

"Hey, baby," he answered.

"You promised dinner here a half hour ago. Should I just call in pizza?"

"I told you that I was taking care of it. I'm only here to help make your life easier," he lied. "I'll be walking in the door in ten minutes. I'm standing at the counter now."

"What are you getting? The kids are starving, and they need to get to bed soon. They have school tomorrow."

"No. I had the ten-piece." Detective Madison imagined that he was straightening out his fictitious food order. "Baby. I got to get this cleared up, but I'm on my way. I'll see you soon." He pressed END before she could say another word. He grabbed his keys to leave.

Detective Johnson smirked. "You wouldn't have that problem if you were single." Detective Johnson constantly teased Detective Madison about how much he enjoyed the single life.

"I can't afford a divorce. I'd sleep here too if I had to go to that hellhole you call an apartment. I'll deal with the wife." Detective Madison gathered his things from his desk. "Do me a favor and break this case before I return in the morning, will you?" he called back to Detective Johnson."

He headed toward the side door to sneak out to his car that he hid from the main entrances. He didn't want to receive any more so-called tips from anyone else.

3 MS. WASHINGTON

Ms. Washington hadn't slept since Sunday, and the delirium was starting to show. With her arms around a rolled-up blanket, she rocked back and forth in her chair while clutching her cell phone. Just like clockwork, she glanced at her phone, hoping for it to ring every five minutes. She hit the screensaver on her phone to re-open the Instagram app. A faint doorbell rang in the distance. She should have stopped scrolling when she heard footsteps, but she didn't.

"She's been like that all day," she heard her son, Junior, say.

Kayla's last Instagram post increased by 200 more comments since she last viewed it five minutes before. She intended to read each one in the hopes of finding more information. The cell phone began to drift from her clutched hand. She followed its movement, startled to see her sister staring at her. There was pity in her eyes. Theresa felt disgusted. She felt dirty somehow. Like her sister looked at her as if she was the one who needed help. Her unemployed, unmarried, welfare-receiving sister looked at her with pity. She couldn't stop her face from turning upside down.

"TT, you have got to get some rest."

"Give me my phone." Theresa tried to snatch the phone from her sister's hand, but she jerked it back right in time.

A river escaped Theresa's eyes. Her upside-down face twisted more in an exercise using each facial muscle. Her sister gave the phone to Junior. She then knelt down to cover Theresa's entire body with hers. She wanted to hug all her problems away. Hug her back to sanity. She held onto Theresa until her loud cry turned into faint sobs, finally convincing her to go into her bedroom to get some rest.

Theresa felt energized as she stretched herself from her bed. She was about to smile, until reality crept back into her mind. Her oldest child and only daughter had been missing for four days. Kayla was glowing Monday morning, as she had always done. She took a quick picture before leaving her room, running down the stairs and out the door, then bouncing down the street toward Harriet Tubman High. That picture was engrained in Theresa's mind because it was the one she studied every five minutes; the most recent picture with growing comments by the second. She looked around the room frantically for her phone, but she didn't see it.

She ran from the room.

"JUNIOR!" she yelled. "Where's my phone?" She looked into the living room, but no one was there. She checked the den and turned to go to Junior's room. *Oh my…* she thought, *what if Junior is missing too.*

"TT," she heard a loud whisper from her sister. She was walking out of the kitchen with a plate in her hand. "Junior is trying to get some rest. He's in his room. Please, come sit. I made y'all some spaghetti."

Theresa thought to herself, *Spaghetti?* How could she eat at a time like this? Why was her sister acting like Kayla wasn't missing? Like someone didn't have her baby girl, doing God knows what, God knows where.

Theresa's face started to wrinkle again. Her sister set the plate down and rushed over to her. She guided her to the dining room table.

"God is with you through this, TT. Just breathe," Theresa's sister said.

Theresa wanted to scream at her, to ask her what kind of God would take her baby girl from her.

People kept acting like Kayla had just run away, but from what? Kayla had a great life. She was smart and popular. Theresa wasn't very strict on her. She had a bunch of friends. Her boyfriend was the school's quarterback, and easily the most handsome young man at the school.

Kayla was so innocent, she thought. So what, she posted pictures in her swimsuit and cropped shirts? At times Kayla would pose with her middle finger up or sticking her tongue out, but how did that make her a slut? She was still a virgin, but Theresa felt that slut was the picture the news was trying to paint of her sweet baby girl.

The newspaper and those dumb detectives took the handful of pictures that could suggest Kayla was a wild child. Somehow, they overlooked the other thousand pictures of her smiling with her friends, eating dinner with the family or getting ready for the football game. Theresa just couldn't understand how anyone could attempt to paint a picture of anything other than perfection of her little girl.

"Where's Junior?" Theresa asked her sister.

"I told you. He's getting rest. Both of you are just so tired because you've been too scared to miss anything. I want both of you to rest. I will answer the phones, cook for you, whatever you need."

Theresa scoffed. "All the things my husband is supposed to do. How could he work at a time like this?"

"You're all just so drained, trying to find any way to cope. Maybe staying busy is what helps him. We're going to get through this. Mom and Dad will be in later tonight."

Theresa hadn't talked to her parents in years, but somehow, she felt comforted knowing that they were coming. It wasn't that she had a problem with her parents. They were just too busy enjoying life and traveling the globe that they didn't have much time for her and her siblings.

"Have you checked her Instagram page?" Theresa asked her sister.

"Yes. I have. She hasn't updated it, nor Snapchat. The only people commenting on her page are those who don't know her personally."

Theresa darted back to the living room. She looked from end table to end table for Detective Madison's business card.

"What are you looking for?"

"I need to call that detective to see if he's heard anything. To see if he has any leads."

"Theresa. You know he'll call you the second he has information."

"No! He's just going to forget about her. I have to call him several times a day to make sure he doesn't forget."

Theresa's sister looked confused, then her face calmed. "Okay. Let me call him. Just sit down and eat, please."

"I'm not hungry."

"Theresa. Please eat. I will tell you what he's said once you're done eating."

Reluctantly, Theresa agreed. She took two bites of spaghetti and a bite of salad to conclude her meal. She walked in on her sister as soon as she ended her call. She stared at her sister, waiting to hear what she had to say, but she didn't speak fast enough. "What did he say?"

"I didn't get to talk to him, but I was able to talk to his partner. A Detective Johnson?"

"Okay," Theresa said impatiently.

"They don't have any further information. They've questioned every one of Kayla's friends. He said the volunteers canvassed her school route and questioned every home in the vicinity. No one has seen her."

"Didn't they trace her cell phone? Has there been any update on that?"

"Still no hits on her cell phone, and no use of her debit card. He assured me that they are still doing everything that they can. He said they review every tip they receive."

Theresa couldn't believe it. That was the same thing Detective Madison had told her that morning. She was starting to think that this was something they made up to tell parents of missing teens.

Theresa's eyes began to well.

"So, what am I supposed to do?"

"The only thing we can do is wait. I'm sure something will come up."

"Call her cell again."

Theresa's sister looked defeated, but did as she was told. No sooner than she put the phone to her ear did she take it away. "Straight to voicemail."

"What if my baby is being raped or tortured, or worse?" Theresa began to wail. Just like before, her sister ran to her aid, showering her with hugs.

Theresa's phone rang. Both sisters jumped. Theresa snatched the phone from her sister's hand and answered it without even looking at the screen.

"Hello? Kayla?" she answered frantically.

"No, it's me, sweetheart." It was her husband, Doug.

"She's still missing, Doug. It's been four days. When will you be home? I can't take this?"

"I'm trying to get off tomorrow so that I can get home a day earlier. Have you been getting any rest?"

"How can I sleep when my daughter is missing? Our daughter is missing?"

"I know, baby. I'm sorry. I'm hurt too. This is not a good time for us to fight."

Theresa held the phone. She knew that her husband was right, but nothing on earth could be pleasing at a time like this. It was like her worst nightmares had come true.

"I talked to Joe, and he said they canvassed the entire neighborhood. They went over the same places that we did Monday and Tuesday, and even started looking outside that area. Everyone knows Kayla's face, so we're sure that they're pretty honest when they say that haven't seen her. I mean, no one has seen her. It's almost like she vanished into thin air," Doug explained.

"I don't know how many more days I can last. I can't. I can't." Theresa felt like her throat was closing up on her.

Her sister snatched the phone away from her. "Doug, we'll call you back." She guided Theresa to the couch to sit. She placed her hand onto each of Theresa's shoulders. "Breathe. Breathe." She repeated this slowly, over and over until Theresa calmed down.

"You're working yourself into an anxiety attack. I know it's really hard, but I need you to try to calm down."

The doorbell rang.

"That has to be Mom and Dad. I'll be right back," Theresa's sister said.

Theresa leaned back into the couch. She looked to the ceiling for answers. Was her sister crazy? How could she calm down? The only thing that would calm her was Kayla walking through that door. Maybe that was Kayla at the door. She jumped to her feet, only to see her sister standing with her parents. She fell back into the couch.

"Oh, baby. I can only imagine how you feel. I'm so sorry that Kayla is missing." Theresa's mom went to sit next to her. She hugged Theresa, but Theresa sat limp.

Her dad took a seat in a nearby chair. "We hear that the police are saying maybe she ran away. Why would she do that?" he asked.

Theresa stared at her dad in disbelief. It's not that she didn't hear what he said, she just couldn't believe he said it, like it was possibly true.

"The news said that she had a fight with her boyfriend and that she told one of her friends she just needed some space. I'm sure she'll show up soon," her mom added.

Who were these people? Theresa thought to herself. She wondered if she came up missing when she was younger, if her parents would have said the same thing. When was the last time they talked to Kayla? They probably didn't know her from a random teenager.

"Why would Kayla run away?" Theresa barely managed.

"You know these kids, honey," her mom started. "We've been following her on the picture book, and she seems to be really popular. One time, she was talking to this BigWeight187 fella and they talked about getting together. Maybe she met up with one of those friends on the picture book. You had your phases honey, remember?"

"Show me," Theresa barked.

Her dad pulled out his phone. He kept staring at it from different angles, as if it was a foreign object. He tapped and scrolled a time or two, returning to his foreign stare. Theresa couldn't take anymore. She always thought she was a respectful child, but there her parents were sitting in her house, accusing her daughter - their granddaughter - of the same things strangers did.

"Here it goes." Her dad finally found what he was looking for.

Theresa stared at the picture of her daughter standing at the bank of the local lake. She stood by a tree and stared innocently at the camera. She remembered the picture vividly because they were spending a family day at the park. Junior took the picture of his sister. She thought it looked professional. She was sure Junior had a future in photography. She blinked away her tears.

Her mom pointed at the conversation on Instagram between Kayla and BigWeight187.

> *BigWeight187 You look like a bad bitch without even trying. We could use your talents in our next video*
>
> *Kayla Talk to my agent*
>
> *BigWeight187* 👀
>
> *BigWeight187 Guaranteed. 1k off top*
>
> *Kayla Bet*

Theresa was confused. She tapped BigWeight187's name to see who he was. His profile read: Bitches and Bricks Coming Soon. She scrolled to see his pictures. The pictures were all of him posing with his thuggish looking friends, half-naked girls, and money. Why would Kayla converse with a guy like this? Did Detective Madison know about this? They said that they had talked to all her friends, but what about people like this?

"I'm sure she's just fine, honey." Her mom placed her hand on Theresa's knee. Theresa looked at her as if she just realized she was there.

"Kayla was so popular and had so many friends that it was easy to miss something like this. Don't blame yourself."

What were her parents saying? Theresa wasn't blaming herself. She would never hurt her kids.

"So, you two think this is my fault?" Theresa eyes shifted back and forth from her mom and dad.

"Kayla had too much freedom. She was dressing like the girls in those videos. We just don't think that's appropriate for a sixteen-year-old."

"Seventeen," Theresa managed through clenched teeth.

"Oh. Yes. Her birthday was just last week," her mom added.

"Your sister told us that you were just driving yourself crazy, so we thought we'd come give you some support." Her mom pulled Theresa into herself.

As furious as Theresa was, she couldn't resist her mom's touch. She leaned her head onto her mom's shoulder. She thought about everything her mom and dad had said. That Kayla could have gone to hang out with friends that she didn't know. It was almost impossible to look at the thousands of comments Kayla received daily on her Instagram pictures. She posted at least three pictures each day. She always had over 2,000 likes on her pictures. What if she did have friends such as BigWeight187 who wanted to meet up with her?

Theresa considered the alternative. What if her parents were right? What if the news was right? What if the detectives were right? She tried to convince herself, but her gut told her different.

4 DEMETRIUS

Saturday was so different. It was unlike the Saturdays that Demetrius had become adjusted to since she had joined the cheerleading squad. She would join Kayla early every Saturday to jog around the park, then they'd finish their run with a smoothie at Sankofa Juice Bar.

Of course, with Kayla missing, Demetrius could go by herself, but it just wasn't the same. She remembered the first day she saw Kayla. She had just moved to the area last year and was so nervous about starting a new school. Kayla was standing near a table, dressed in her cheerleading uniform. Her waist length hair was pulled up into a top ponytail, while her edges were slicked into little swirls on each side. Her cheer uniform seemed to fit her like a glove. The other cheerleaders looked like teenagers in their uniforms, but Kayla was built like a grown woman. Her belly button peeked out from her cropped top as she outstretched the flier to Demetrius. A perfect pearly smile spread across Kayla's dazzling face. The way Kayla's eyes shined while asking Demetrius to come to tryouts made Demetrius feel like she was the only person in the world. How could someone as perfect as Kayla treat a dork such as Demetrius so nicely?

Demetrius was slow to trust people because everyone seemed like a bully at the school that she had barely escaped from. They made fun of her skin tone, height, weight, her braces, pimples, glasses anything else they could find. She was reluctant to take the flier from Kayla because she thought she was imagining it. Demetrius looked around her to make sure this wasn't one of those mean girl tricks that she had become all too familiar with.

"Are you talking to me?" Demetrius asked Kayla.

Kayla giggled. Demetrius was starting to think it was a joke again. That Kayla's friendly smile would turn into an evil grin in just a matter of seconds.

"Of course. You're new here, right? I'd like you to give cheer a try before anyone else tries to snatch you up."

Demetrius knew that it was a joke. Before someone else snatched her up? Who would want her?

"No, no. I'm too big to be a cheerleader." Demetrius had already imagined herself being the butt of the entire cheerleading squad's joke. "Besides, I have no coordination." She gave Kayla back the flier.

Kayla simply looked at the flier. "There's no such thing as too big. All you need is a positive attitude. I bet you'll fall in love with it," Kayla reassured her.

Demetrius stared into Kayla's eyes and didn't see the joke. She didn't see the evil grin forming. Her past had told her different, but she promised her mom that she'd try to look for the good in people instead of only seeing the evil.

"Okay. I'll come. Please be nice to me." That last part just slipped out.

"I promise you. You won't regret it." Kayla said it with so much confidence that Demetrius felt like she could trust Kayla with her life. And Kayla was right; Demetrius didn't regret it. She often looked back at that day as the best day of her life.

Demetrius often thought of herself as one of Kayla's best friends. Of course, there was Tiffany, who had been her friend since junior high. Then there was Jenna, but she had only been her friend for about a month since she was now the new girl. When Jenna first came, Demetrius was worried that Jenna would replace her. She thought that was her newest competition, but Kayla never missed their run. She smiled, thinking that was why Kayla was such a great friend. She was super popular, very smart and found time to be a great friend to all three of them. Everyone seemed happy with Kayla.

She really hoped Kayla was simply doing something out of character and not actually missing. When she didn't see Kayla in class Monday afternoon, she thought maybe she had left for a doctor appointment. When Demetrius texted her after school and didn't receive an answer, she figured maybe Kayla had gotten as busy as she had with school work that evening. Demetrius didn't realize something was up until she saw Kayla's mom walking down the school hallway crying.

Ms. Washington ran up to Demetrius as soon as she saw her. "Have you seen Kayla?" she questioned.

"No ma'am," Demetrius responded. "I haven't seen her since lunch yesterday."

"She didn't come home last night. I have no idea where she is."

The counselor ran up to Ms. Washington and ushered her to continue down the hallway. Demetrius stood there alone, wondering what was happening. She took out her phone to call Kayla, but the phone went straight to voicemail. *That was odd.* Kayla never let her phone die. She texted her. *Where RU?*

Demetrius waited a few seconds, but there was no response. She suddenly realized that she was already late for class and hurried on. After Demetrius was settled in class, she texted Jenna and Tiffany. *Have you seen Kayla?*

Jenna responded, *Nope.*

Tiffany responded thirty minutes later, *You mean since she vowed that she'd never speak to me again?*

Huh? Demetrius thought. *When did Kayla say that?* She ignored her comment. Demetrius responded to each of them: *Her mom is crying. She said she didn't come home last night.*

Jenna responded, *Wow.*

Tiffany responded. *Are you serious?* Followed by: *Her phone is going straight to voicemail. That's not like her.*

Demetrius couldn't wait to get to lunch that day, but in the short three hours it took for lunch to start, all 1,500 students had heard about Kayla's disappearance and had already crafted stories of where she was. Demetrius, Jenna and Tiffany barely had a chance to speak in private due to all the bum-rushed questions.

The girls met in the bathroom moments before lunch ended.

"Where could she be?" Tiffany pondered.

"You and Brian probably ran her off," Jenna stated.

"How many times do I have to tell you, there is nothing going on between me and Brian?"

"Have either of you talked to him? Do you know if he knows?" Demetrius asked.

"After that fight they had yesterday. I bet he knows," Jenna scoffed. Demetrius didn't like the sound of that.

"Tiffany, don't you have your next class with him? Can you ask him?"

Tiffany stared at the floor and shook her head slowly. Demetrius didn't understand what was happening, but there wasn't enough time to figure it out. She grabbed her phone to speed dial Kayla again. Same thing. Straight to voicemail.

"Jenna, can you ask Brian if you see him before I do?"

"Doesn't Tiffany have his number?" Jenna said sarcastically. "I'm sure she'll be in class today. She's probably just hanging out. You're really blowing this out of proportion. I need to head to class." Jenna left the bathroom.

Tiffany finally lifted her head. "Look, I have to go to class too. I'll keep an ear out and let you know if I hear anything."

Demetrius flashed Tiffany a weak smile and watched her walk out of the bathroom, then she heard the bell ring.

Demetrius opened the Instagram app to see if Kayla had updated any of her posts. Kayla's Monday morning smile gleamed back at her. Demetrius's stomach churned. Kayla took a good morning picture every morning, but there was no new picture. She speed-dialed Kayla again. Straight to voicemail. *Damn.*

She thought back to the conversation she'd just had with Jenna and Tiffany. Something was weird between them, but then, again something had been weird between them since Jenna came to the school. Demetrius had always brushed it off as new girl jealousy. When Jenna first came, she felt the same, so she thought it would soon pass with Tiffany.

Demetrius had no idea where Kayla could be. She didn't realize it was such a big deal until she was questioned by Principal McNair. Now, Kayla had been missing for five days and there was no sign of her in sight. Demetrius was really trying to be calm about the whole thing, but the Saturday run was always a staple, and it wasn't just the run. There were no good morning posts. The band of followers that Kayla had begun to post #whereskayla hashtags. The police were involved, and now she finally understood what was up with Jenna and Tiffany.

She should have realized that something was up all along, but Demetrius wasn't the most attentive person. She really just wanted everyone else to join on her newfound happiness since she came to Harriet Tubman High. Jenna claimed that Tiffany had been messing with Brian behind Kayla's back. Brian could be a bit of a bad boy, but Demetrius never thought he would actually mess with Kayla's best friend. They used to hang out with Brian all the time.

After their bathroom talk, Jenna gave Demetrius her theory. She explained that Brian had been pressuring Kayla to have sex lately and maybe that him cheating with Tiffany was a way for him to get back at Kayla. Demetrius was so confused because although she knew that Tiffany was a flirt, she had never seen her flirt with Brian.

Demetrius felt like her band of friends was falling apart. She barely talked with Tiffany and had only talked with Jenna a few times since Kayla's disappearance. Just a couple of weeks ago, it was always the four of them: Kayla, Jenna, Tiffany, and Demetrius. They ate lunch together. Texted each other all day during class. Hung out at cheer practice after school. Jenna wasn't a cheerleader like the other three, but she was there right along with them.

The first time Demetrius thought that something must've been up was two weeks before. It was after cheer practice. Kayla was giving Demetrius tips on the new cheer routine when Jenna approached them from the bleachers.

"How long have Brian and Tiffany been that close?" Jenna stared into the distance. Demetrius and Kayla followed her gaze. About fifty feet away, Tiffany was talking to Brian. They were both smiling and laughing.

"What do you mean?" Kayla asked. "They're supposed to be friends. Brian and I have been together since freshman year. Any friend of mine is a friend of Tiffany's."

"I can tell by their body language that they may be more than just friends," Jenna said with an accusatory tone.

Kayla laughed. "Jenna, you are such a conspiracy theorist. If you want to conspire something, we need to figure out how to get you on this team in mid-season."

Demetrius had never thought that anyone would try to get with Brian. The entire school knew that Brian and Kayla were sweethearts. Matter of fact, the whole city knew. Everyone who was close to Kayla was branded on her Instagram page. Kayla didn't seem to question Tiffany and Brian's relationship, so why should she? A few days after that incident, Demetrius realized that she had hardly seen Tiffany and Jenna around at the same time.

Sitting on her balcony, Demetrius reluctantly scrolled down Kayla's Instagram page. She was trying not to throw herself into this #whereskayla fiasco. Jenna was sure that Kayla was fine. Tiffany was really scared. Brian wasn't around them anymore. It was like the rumor of he and Tiffany's relationship stopped him from talking to either of them.

Demetrius felt like she was on an island. This was a time that the three of them should come together to retrace Kayla's last appearance, but instead, it felt like they were distant enemies. Even if Kayla came back, Demetrius wondered if they would ever be able to mend their relationship; if Brian, Jenna, and Tiffany would all be friends. Demetrius smiled; Kayla was their glue. If Jenna was right, her mini personal vacation should be over by the start of school Monday. She would glue them all back together. Demetrius's smile faded. Maybe she was simply being naïve again.

5 JUSTJESS

Kayla was the most gorgeous person in the city of Garvey. She was a local celebrity. Everyone followed her IG page. All the guys wanted to date her, and all the girls wanted to be just like her, even girls who didn't share her flawless caramel brown skin, almond eyes, high cheekbones, and full lips. JustJess thought she and Kayla could be twins, though. They had a lot in common. She decided to follow everything that Kayla did because she knew Kayla was going to be a success. That was the reason why she started the where's Kayla hashtag.

She knew something was up when Kayla skipped her midday selfie. JustJess expected to see something about cheer practice, BFFTiff, BFFDede, or anything about her juicy star football player boyfriend. JustJess wanted the same exact life that Kayla had the cool awkward looking best friends, the gorgeous GQ model boyfriend, the constant A's, perfect cheer jumps, nice little brother - everything. Kayla was perfect, and JustJess was dying to know where she was.

JustJess remembered the day that she finally saw Kayla in person.

She tried to casually walk up to her on accident, but couldn't help but sound like a fan. Kayla seemed disinterested, until she told her that she followed her on Instagram. She asked for a picture and Kayla happily complied. Just as JustJess pictured her: a nice girl, happy to pose with her fans.

JustJess bought the same makeup as Kayla. She watched makeup tutorials to try to get the same glow as Kayla. She almost achieved the look, but the hair was another thing. There was no way JustJess could afford bundles. She couldn't work as much as she wanted to because of school, and there was no way her parents would allow it.

"You spent $50 on what!" her dad exclaimed when he found out she had bought new makeup.

JustJess tried to explain to her dad over and over again why makeup was an investment, and not a waste. There was no way he would allow her to buy $300 bundles, even if she took extra shifts for it. He just didn't understand. She saw how Kayla went from a regular high school girl to an Instagram celebrity. She was receiving endorsement deals, and that was JustJess's goal. The $100 eyelash extensions that she planned to get that weekend would help.

Every day JustJess would post on Kayla's page and her own, questioning #whereskayla. She'd post about her favorite Kayla pictures and what she missed most about her. She had even started a countdown.

It's been 7Days #whereskayla I hope she returns to school tomorrow. JustJess posted on Kayla's Monday morning post.

She examined Kayla's flashy smile that she had become so familiar with. Her hair was combed effortlessly into a bun, covered with her favorite filtered flower crown. Her eyebrows were arched perfectly with just a tint of mascara grazing her eyelashes. Her simple dimple-indented squared cheeks. JustJess looked at the image closer. Kayla didn't have that same eye twinkle that she normally had. JustJess knew the traces of Kayla's face like no one else. She had to. How else could she replicate her image if she didn't?

JustJess wondered why she didn't notice it before. Maybe something was bothering Kayla Monday morning before she left for school. She backtracked through Kayla's pictures to determine when her perfectly happy smile disappeared.

Sunday night, Kayla posted a photo of her dinner. Chicken, peas, and salad. The caption read, Dinner with the fam. 2,016 likes. That was normal.

JustJess scrolled to the next picture. Kayla was lying on her bed. Her hair resembled a huge crown flowing around her head. JustJess knew that it was Kayla's bed because she saw the purple bedspread, and in the corner of the photo was Kayla's favorite pillow; it was purple and lined in gold. Kayla used a filter that made the picture look soft. That was typical for a bedroom picture. Kayla looked calm through squinted bedroom eyes. JustJess couldn't tell if the look on her face was sadness or boredom. The caption read: I just want to lie in bed all day. *That could mean anything,* JustJess thought. She could have been tired from her epic surprise birthday party she had that Saturday. 4,432 likes.

Sunday morning, she took a selfie, but it only included her head and shoulders. Her face was serious. The caption read: *Model pose.* It was hard to tell if Kayla was happy in that picture because she was trying so hard to be serious. She used JustJess's favorite filter. It was a cross between a soft picture and an illustration. It really outlined the sharp edges in the photo. Kayla wore purple shirt. 2,382 likes.

JustJess scrolled to the next image. It was a collage from Saturday night. Half of Kayla's favorite people were in the photos. One picture was of Kayla dressed in a purple, skin-tight cut-out dress. She was kissing BFFTiff on her cheek. BFFTiff was staring at the camera smiling. The next image was of Kayla and BFBrian. The picture caught BFBrian holding Kayla in midair. Both of them had smiles plastered across their faces.

The last picture in the collage showed Kayla with her arms around a girl that JustJess had never seen before. Even though the picture was taken in a dark room, JustJess could tell by the girl's pencil thin legs that she was in need of a tan. JustJess made the image larger so that she could see the girl. She couldn't make out the girl's face because her head was thrown back in laughter. The party must have been a lot of fun. Kayla's arm was around the girl, but she was focused on teasing the camera with her millionaire smile. The girl's hair was long like Kayla's, but it was jet black and bone straight. The girl's jacket covered her silky shirt. JustJess continued to look over the mystery girl and saw that she wore Kayla's #shoeporn shoe. They were $1,000 shoes. Kayla posted #shoeporn often, but these shoes she posted several times. A different color each time.

Interesting. JustJess thought. She looked at the caption. It read:

> #itsmybirthdaybitch *BFFTiff BFBrian BFFJen We miss you BFFDede?*

That girl must have been BFFJen. When did Kayla make this new friend? JustJess almost felt betrayed because she thought she knew everything about Kayla. JustJess scrolled to read the comments.

> **Shaylakay** #whereskayla *She looks so happy in these pictures*
>
> **Toofly** #whereskayla *That night was epic. She definitely went out with a bang.*
>
> **Jasoncarter** #whereskayla *She was the best. I hope she resurfaces.*

JustJess was happy to see that people were using her hashtag. She continued to scroll.

> **Dynamicduo** *This is when it all went left.* #whereskayla
>
> **BikerGirl** #whereskayla *Tiffany is no best friend and Brian is a snob. I heard he was abusive too.* #Whenyourfriendsareyourenemies

What? JustJess was confused. She felt like she missed something. She saw that the comments were just left on Saturday. She needed more information. JustJess immediately clicked the reply button below BikerGirl's post. *Why do you say that?* she typed.

She tapped on the reply button beneath Dynamicduo. *Why'd it go left?* she typed.

Here she thought she was Kayla's number one fan, but she had no idea what was going on. She remembered watching a few snapchat videos from the party, but everything looked normal. Just a bunch of dancing, loud music, drinking, and partying.

Her phone chirped. She stared at the reply from Dynamicduo. *BFBrian and BFFTiff decided to mess around right there at Kayla's birthday party. She caught them in the act. That's one hell of a gift.*

"What!" JustJess exclaimed.

"What's wrong, baby?" her mom asked. JustJess was so lost in her search for Kayla that she forgot she was sitting in the living room with her mom. Her mom was fixated on the television, while JustJess was focused on her phone.

"Oh nothing, Mom." She didn't want to tell her mom that she was looking into Kayla's disappearance. Her mom hinted to her several times before that she thought she was becoming obsessive.

JustJess returned to the photo. She guessed that Bikergirl wasn't going to respond. JustJess went to Brian's Instagram page. His page was public, so she knew that she could do some snooping there. Nothing came up. She thought for a second. She knew that she hadn't made a mistake. She frequently checked his page, it should have been there. Unless of course he deactivated it. Now, JustJess was really interested in what could have happened.

She went to Tiffany's page, but already knew that she wouldn't have luck. Tiffany's page was private. She tried to request her months ago, but Tiffany never accepted. JustJess wasn't sure why Tiffany was so private. She didn't even have a quarter of the followers that Kayla had, but whatever.

JustJess went back to Kayla's Monday picture. She was going to study each of the comments to see if she could figure out what happened. This story was developing right under her nose. She always thought that she'd be the first to actually find out what happened with Kayla, so she had to jump on top of the developing story quickly. The picture likes had increased to 10,232. This didn't surprise JustJess. The first picture was receiving additional likes regularly since she started the #whereskayla on the Tuesday after her disappearance. When the Garvey Morning News story came out Thursday morning, the likes had doubled overnight.

JustJess looked at the comments. They were increasing right before her eyes. She knew this research was going to cost her a few hours, but it wasn't like she hadn't spent that much time before. After an hour of reading comments and replies, JustJess felt that she finally had an understanding of what could have happened to Kayla. It did seem like she may have run away to save face. She posted pictures of her, Brian, Tiffany and Dede every week for years. JustJess could only imagine how devastating it was to see Brian and Tiffany having sex at her 17th birthday party. Brian was the one who threw the surprise party. He could have at least waited until the party was over. JustJess went from loving BFBrian to thinking that he was a piece of shit.

JustJess needed more intel. She left the living room. She needed the privacy of her bedroom to find out more information. The look of her mattress on the floor always knocked her energy down a few notches. Why couldn't she have a big poster bed like Kayla? At least she had a purple comforter. She plopped on her bed and dialed her cousin. She had to know more about what was going on because she attended Harriet Tubman High.

"What's up, Jo!"

"Hey, Jess."

"So… I was looking at Kayla's Instagram and I wanted to know if you had heard anything about Brian and Tiffany messing around."

Jo laughed. "You have always been so obsessed with that girl. Have you asked your mom if you can attend Harriet Tubman next year? My mom said you can use our address."

JustJess wanted nothing more than to attend school with her idol. She could be BFFJess. But, she shook her dream away to focus on her call. "Instagram has come up with a string of things that happened at her birthday party. I even heard that she had a fight with Brian right before she came up missing."

"Yea, I heard that too," Jo replied.

"So, what are people saying around the school?"

"I heard the same thing on Friday. I'll start asking around tomorrow and let you know what I find out."

"Text me as soon as you find out," JustJess pleaded.

6 JUNIOR

Junior couldn't believe that his sister was still missing. She was so annoying to him. Always taking selfies and forcing him to be her photographer anytime she saw him around. He thought it was so dumb of her to be obsessed with what other people thought, but with every passing day, he was beginning to regret ever feeling that way. He could only hope that she swung by his room telling him she needed a few pics. She always said a few pics, but it was never just a few.

Junior's most hated picture of his sister was the one he took of her by the park. It was not unusual for him to take picture after picture of his sister, but that day he swore he took at least a hundred. Every time he stopped to show her the pictures she'd find a new complaint.

You didn't get the light right. No, that's a bad angle. I'm sorry, that wasn't the smile I intended to use. Those were just some of the things she'd say. He was so upset with her that evening he vowed not to ever take another picture of her again. He told her he'd throw her phone the moment she gave it to him. She apologized to him profusely and started taking more selfies. She would tell him that he was such a great photographer and that her pictures were never as good as his.

It took weeks before he considered forgiving his sister, but it wasn't until she walked into his room and handed him a fifty-dollar bill that he had an incentive to no longer be mad.

"What's this for?" he asked.

"All of your hard work, it's starting to pay off," she said as she sat on his bed. Her lips curved into a huge smile.

"Where'd you get this?" Junior had never held a fifty-dollar bill before. He felt rich. He sat up in his bed. She had his full attention.

"My pictures are making me money. Well, your pictures are making me money and as long as I make money, I can pay you as my photographer. But you have to promise not to tell anyone."

Telling someone was the last thing on Junior's mind. He knew that if his mom knew he had money, she would watch every penny he spent. She'd even make him save some of it. He wasn't telling anyone about the fifty-dollars. Now that Kayla was promising him more money, he couldn't wait to take more photos of her.

"Do you want to take more pictures now?" He asked ecstatically, overjoyed with the possibility of making more money.

Kayla laughed and stood to leave. "No, not right now. But we will soon." She shut the door behind her as she left out the room.

That had to have been about three weeks ago, two weeks before

Kayla went missing. Since then, she had given him another two-hundred dollars for his services. He wondered if this was already the end of his photography career. If he wasn't taking pictures of Kayla, he didn't want to take pictures of anyone else.

Kayla was missing. Junior felt horrible about it, but had to keep himself together. His mom was completely depressed. She spent most of her time crying, sleeping, and harassing the detectives. He felt like he had to be strong for her. He thought if she saw him crying, she'd start back crying too.

When Junior's dad wasn't working, he was at home looking like a lost puppy. He tried to spend time with Junior and keep them both busy doing odd jobs around the house, but Junior could tell that it was wearing on him too. His dad looked like he had aged a decade over the last week. He'd catch his dad yelling at someone on the phone when he thought Junior was away in his room. He'd also caught his dad crying a few times too. The only people who seemed somewhat normal were his grandparents.

He had never spent this much time with his grandparents before, but it seemed like they weren't planning to leave until Kayla returned. He was grateful for that, as he felt some sense of normalcy with them. They'd take him to the movies or to the arcade to play games. Anything so that he didn't have to think about what was going on. One or both of them made sure he had someone to talk to, and that he always had something to eat. When one of them felt like he was in a good space to receive information, they would give him regular updates on what had been done in search of his sister. Junior really felt a part of the family with them around.

It had been a week since his sister kissed him on her way out of the door to go to school. That was the last time he had seen her. She looked happy, but he knew better. Something had happened with Kayla after her birthday party. He wasn't sure what it was, but he knew something wasn't the same.

She tried to hide her tears from him Sunday morning when he went to ask her if she was going to come eat breakfast. She assured him that she wasn't crying, that she just wasn't feeling well. Deep down, he knew better. She didn't come out of the room at all that day, until she snuck out the backdoor later that evening.

Junior didn't know when she had snuck out. All he remembered was that an hour after their parents left for the store, the doorbell rang. Junior was focused on his video game, so he ignored it until the third ring. He knew that whoever it was, it had to have been someone for Kayla. When she didn't answer it, he opened the door, startled to see Brian's angry face. Junior was in shock and just stood there staring at him.

"Where's Kayla?" Brian barked.

Junior shook at the sound of his voice, but he didn't move. Brian's face was all mangled and dark. His eyes were blood shot red. Junior could have sworn he saw steam releasing from his ears.

"Junior!" Brian yelled, "Where's your sister?"

"Um. Wait, I'll go find her." Without thinking, Junior slammed the door shut. It was a habit to not let Brian in because he and Junior's dad didn't always get along. Brian usually felt more comfortable on the porch anyway. Junior called for Kayla, but she didn't answer. He searched her room and the bathroom, but she was nowhere to be found. He checked his parents' room and the kitchen, just to be sure before returning to the front door to tell Brian that she wasn't there. He figured that she must have snuck out. It wasn't his business, but she had done that a few times over the last couple of weeks. It didn't bother him because she was always gone only a few hours.

Junior wasn't sure when she slid back in. He continued playing his video game until dinner that night, when she joined the family at the table as if she'd never left.

Junior didn't tell anyone about her behavior. He thought it was teenage girl stuff that didn't have anything to do with her disappearance. He remembered when he was six, he'd find Kayla crying all of the time. She looked different then. Her big hair would rest on her shoulders and she never wore makeup. They were a lot closer then. They would wear matching T-shirts and basketball shorts. His dad used to tease Kayla about being so simple. He often bought Kayla and Junior's clothing and shoes at the same store. They'd wear the same outfit, in two different sizes, but that was then. Now, Junior couldn't even name a store where Kayla shopped.

Even though he and his sister no longer wore matching outfits or chased one another around the park, he still felt close to her. They would talk to each other every day, and hardly ever fought. From what he'd heard from his friends, it was normal for teenage girls to start acting really weird. Out of the blue, she started dressing girly and wearing her hair super long. That's why he was happy she became closer to her friends, as he had no interest in those things. He overheard her talking with her friends about boys and cycles before, and he didn't want to discuss those things. For him, it was better that she kept some of those things to herself.

Now with Kayla gone, he felt his family slowly falling apart. His dad surmised that Kayla ran away, and began convincing Junior of the same. His parents would argue every time they were together because his mom remained adamant that her daughter did not run away. She felt in her gut that Kayla was in danger.

He wished he had talked to Kayla more. Maybe those things in her private life would explain why she had run away - if she had indeed, run away.

Junior brushed his teeth to get ready for school. He looked around the bathroom aimlessly while cleaning his teeth, until his eyes landed on Kayla's caboodles. At least, that was what she had called the cases that housed the creams and colors, and just everything she put on her face. Kayla had three of them. It would take her hours to get ready each morning, so she'd wake up way before his alarm clock would go off. It only took Junior ten minutes to get ready, and watching her toil away each morning made him happy to be a boy. He couldn't imagine using that much time in the bathroom. He finished brushing his teeth, casting one last glance towards Kayla's things before hurrying out the bathroom door.

Junior was surprised the detective was sitting in the living room with his mom and grandparents. He stopped to listen. His grandmother was sitting next to his mom on the couch. She had her hand on his mom's shoulder. His mom was shaking her head. As soon as his grandfather noticed him, he scurried to him.

"Hey, kid. Are you ready for school?" his grandfather asked.

"What's going on?" Junior inquired, but instead of an answer his grandfather ushered him outside. They walked the four blocks to school in silence. Junior didn't need a chaperone, but he welcomed the company.

Finally his grandfather said, "The detectives do not suspect foul play in your sister's disappearance. They still think she's a runaway. Detective Madison is giving us some information about services that help with missing loved ones, but he says that there's not much else that he can do."

Junior didn't know how he felt about the information that his grandfather gave him. His grandfather seemed pretty calm about the news, so he figured he should be calm too. "What do you think about that?"

"I really don't know what to think," his grandfather said.

His grandfather's response reassured him some. Junior often didn't know much about the rumors that people said about his sister. He just knew that he missed her. At first, he was really scared just like his mom was. Then, he thought that maybe Kayla was just upset about something and had run away as his dad suspected. Now he just didn't know what to think. He felt like he and his grandfather may have been on the same page.

Junior stopped walking. "Granddad. I heard that Kayla had a fight with Brian before she came up missing. Do you think he did something to her?"

His grandfather looked concerned. "Where'd you hear that?"

"That's what the people at school were saying Friday." Junior remembered Brian's facial expression on the Sunday before Kayla's disappearance. "I heard that Brian could sometimes be mean, but I always thought Brian was a nice person. Do you think he would hurt her?"

His grandfather looked around. He seemed to be thinking. "Maybe you shouldn't go to school today Junior. What do you think about that?"

Junior was surprised. That wasn't the answer he expected, but he liked it nonetheless. "Sure!" Junior exclaimed. He turned around to start walking back to his house.

"Let's walk and talk a bit before we go , shall we?"

"Uhm, okay." Junior didn't understand what was going on, but he was happy not to go to school. He was getting tired of the kids there asking him about his sister anyway. Some of the bigger kids had Instagram pages, and they were stopping him in the hallway to discover what he knew.

Junior would often shrug and say *I guess she ran away*, but that was because he kept thinking that his sister would be back soon. After an entire week without her, he was becoming more worried. If she could just call him to say she was fine, he thought he'd feel better about it.

"There are a lot of rumors about Kayla and her friends. We have talked to all of them several times. All her friends returned to class immediately after lunch and, for the most part their stories are the same. She was the only one who didn't return to class. She's a really smart girl and she's seventeen now. We can only hope that she knows what she is doing."

"You're right Granddad," Junior said, although he didn't completely agree. How could Kayla leave and not take her three caboodles of face stuff? That face stuff seemed really important to her. His mom was in Kayla's room rambling almost every day and said that nothing was out of place. She didn't notice any clothes missing or anything. Junior felt himself getting worried again.

"Granddad?" Junior said. "Can we go to the movies today?"

His grandfather smiled. "Sure thing, son."

7 MELISSA

"Where's my new model for AVO swimwear?" Melissa's boss was annoying her about the new assignment.

Melissa dropped four profile pictures onto her desk for her boss to see. "Pick one," she said.

He looked at the images disapprovingly. One picture was of a perfectly tanned teen with smooth, toned beanstalk legs. Her flowing hair was blowing in the wind. She looked like a lingerie model.

The next picture was of a thin, dark-skinned girl with thick, curly hair that was manicured like a shrub. Her innocent brown eyes made her seem easily approachable.

Another picture was of a lily-white girl with cropped blond curls. She had piercing blue eyes and wore a cunning smirk.

The last picture was of an Indian girl, with shapely hips. Her stark black hair seemed endless, brushing against her flawless natural face.

"Where's the Black doll?"

"Missing."

"Well, find her. Get her on the phone. I told you weeks ago that I had made my choice. These girls are gorgeous, but they don't bring the innocent diverse teen image that I need for this swim line."

"You don't understand. She is missing. She hasn't updated her IG account since last Monday. No one knows where she is. They think she ran away."

"Well, did you call her?"

"I called her. Her friends have called her. No one knows where she is. I've been studying her page since she missed our meeting on Friday. She doesn't seem to be resurfacing anytime soon."

"SHIT. And this is the best you can do, Melissa?" her boss asked, pointing at the photos on her desk. "Millions of Instagram accounts, and you can't find what I'm looking for."

"I just haven't had the time. I was sold on her, just like you were. I'll get back to it now."

Her boss stormed out of her office. Melissa had never had this problem before. These young girls always answered enthusiastically when she reached out to them for an endorsement deal. They usually had signed papers back to her within an hour. Melissa was the best agent at Brand Images, and she'd always delivered exactly what the owners wanted. She never thought her ideal client would disappear.

That type of thing just didn't happen.

Melissa's boss was a self-made millionaire. He always said that innovation and spontaneity were the tools to his success. He was a born hustler. He started with convincing his Instagram-addicted sister to model for his friend's T-shirt line. When he saw the money trickle in, he knew he had a good idea. Melissa was just happy she was the first person he hired. As long as the money kept rolling, her boss didn't mind sharing the wealth by giving hefty bonuses.

Melissa's job was to scour social media sites to find specific models to accentuate a company's image. It was an awesome job, and she was good at it. She knew what look she needed for which brand and found it immediately. The first time she came across Kayla's page was about a month before. She was at Neiman Marcus, modeling a pair Louboutin shoes. The caption read: #Iwish #neimans #shoeporn. Kayla's look outshined that of the expensive designer shoes. Melissa was blown away by the fact that the girl was in love with the camera, had seemingly perfect pictures, and above all, she had more than 20,000 followers.

Kayla wasn't just a girl that posed for the 'gram. She was a friend, a student, a girlfriend, and a daughter that everyone seemed to love. She seemed like the type of girl that other young girls strived to be. She had already booked Kayla for two small jobs before that were extremely successful, so the meeting Friday was to discuss the additional ten jobs that Melissa had lined up.

Instagram modeling wasn't a long-term job for the mini models, but it was for Melissa. She could easily get a model a few dozen gigs before finding someone new. That's what her clients wanted. Fresh, cool faces making their products seem like a household necessity. She had no clue how to find a girl like Kayla. She sold her clients tailored girls. She did extensive research on their page and surroundings to make sure they would be a good fit. Once the clients agreed, she took the guarantee to the model. It really was a quick process and beneficial for all parties involved. She never had an upset model or client. She was on a roll, but now her roll seemed to have slowed.

Melissa did a search on her computer to check for any recent signs of Kayla. There were no new stories and no coverage on Kayla. If Melissa didn't know any better, she'd swear that she made Kayla up. She searched for the most recent #whereskayla. A picture emerged. The picture was a single photo that featured a girl who appeared to be Kayla.

She donned Kayla's wavy, waist-length hair and big smile. Her eyes were hidden behind oversized shades. Her purple cropped shirt rested above her belly button. Her dark denim jeans firmly exposed her growing curves. Two purple and rhinestone stiletto fingernails dazzled at the end of the peace sign she made. She leaned against a brick wall. One of her feet stood away from the other. Kayla was wearing the same Louboutin shoes that she wore in the Neiman's store, but she was no longer in the store; she was outside. It was hard to tell anything definite in the picture other than the fact that the picture was taken outside, against a wall.

Melissa clicked the picture to review the original post. The picture was posted by a guy named Lowkeyboss. The caption read: *Wherever you are I hope you're having fun. That beautiful smile could paint the world. #badbitchstatus #lowkeybossbitch #whereskayla*.

The likes and comments were growing by the second. Melissa clicked on the comments to see if she could find out when the picture was taken. According to Lowkeyboss, he hung out with Kayla and a few friends on Sunday. He said she was fine then. It seemed like the post was gaining a lot of attention. The response feed seemed to last forever.

Melissa realized she was getting lost. It was a rule of hers. If it wasn't pertaining to booking a client or a model, she couldn't waste any time on it. It was clear that Kayla was not around, and a new girl had to be found by the end of the day. She returned to her search results and saw another picture of Kayla with another girl, a girl who looked like she could be Kayla's sister. Melissa clicked on the picture to view the source.

The picture was posted by JustJess. JustJess's arm was outstretched. It was obvious that she was the one who took the selfie. Both girls smiled into the camera. The caption read: *I'm so happy to have met you. I hope you're living your dreams. #myinspiration #whereskayla #harriettubmanhigh #cheerleader*

Melissa clicked on JustJess's profile picture to look at her other photos. JustJess's perfectly contoured face could be seen in class, at the park, and hanging with her friends. She had the look that Melissa was going for, but her pictures were hit and miss. She hardly had any full body images. She lacked the extra-curricular images, family pictures, and just general charm that Kayla had. To make it even worse, she only had 2,000 followers. Melissa couldn't believe the luck she was having.

She clicked on the #harriettubmanhigh to see if it would lead her to any ideal students that could fit the description, but all she could find were comments and rumors about Kayla. A new hashtag was started by the Tubman students. They posted #principalmcnair to encourage the principal to create a memorial for Kayla. Melissa thought these kids were going to take over the internet with their hashtags. Although popular students were the least expensive models, Melissa was not inspired by the empty images. It was back to the drawing board. She had to pursue a new plan.

8 PRINCIPAL MCNAIR

Kayla's disappearance was the worst thing that could have happened to Harriet Tubman High School. Principal McNair was having a difficult time figuring out how to deal with losing his best student, calming his student body of 1,500, and dodging a Public Relations nightmare. Everybody wanted answers, and he had none.

As soon as Ms. Washington ran into the school crying the previous Tuesday morning, Principal McNair was at a loss for words. He felt sorry for the upset Ms. Washington, but he thought it had nothing to do with him or his school. That is, until he looked at the attendance records and saw that Kayla had only missed the classes after lunch. He didn't tell Ms. Washington that he was concerned. He had the counselor simply console her and guide her to a secluded office to alleviate her anxiety.

Principal McNair performed his due diligence by quietly talking to each teacher that was on Kayla's schedule for the day. The teachers explained to him that it was a normal day for Kayla. Nothing seemed out of the ordinary. The teachers who taught the classes she missed also didn't think anything was wrong. She didn't attend class, so they just figured she was absent, not missing.

Satisfied with each teacher's answer, Principal McNair didn't think any more of it. The next day, Kayla's dad, Doug Carlisle greeted him as he parked that Wednesday morning. He could see the distress on Mr. Carlisle's face. Wasting no time, Kayla's dad explained that he wanted to search the school. Principal McNair's first thought was, *no way*, but the look of exhaustion on Mr. Carlisle's face stopped him. Instead, he said, "I can't authorize a full search without probable cause, but we can check around before school starts if you'd like."

Mr. Carlisle seemed so grateful. He explained that they had talked to each of Kayla's friends and concluded that she came up missing after a disagreement after lunch. Principal McNair had no knowledge of a disagreement. He made a mental note to find out more about it as soon as Mr. Carlisle left.

They only had enough time to fully search one floor. When the staff and students began to trickle in, Principal McNair calmly advised Mr. Carlisle that they'd have to stop because he didn't want to alarm anyone. He told him that he could return after school and they could search more if he'd like. Mr. Carlisle agreed. Principal McNair thought he looked a bit more relieved after his search. His worry had been replaced with a look of determination. Mr. Carlisle shook the principal's hand and thanked him before he left.

Principal McNair called the counselor into his office after assuring her it wouldn't take long. He didn't want to discuss Kayla unless it was behind closed doors. Students were known to blow things out of proportion.

"It appears that Kayla Carlisle is still missing. How was her mom when she left yesterday?"

"I haven't see someone that upset since…" she thought a moment, "I don't think I ever have. She's going crazy looking for Kayla. Is she really missing?"

"Her dad just left. He wanted to search the school to see if maybe she was still here. Apparently, a few of her friends said there was an altercation in the cafeteria Monday before she came up missing. I want to get ahead of this thing. Can you send each of her friends to my office? I want to see them one by one, but I don't want them to have a chance to talk to each other before I talk to them."

"Of course, Principal," the counselor assured him before leaving his office.

Principal McNair told his secretary that he had to talk to a few students that morning, and to hold all calls and meetings until he advised her that he was done.

Twenty minutes after the first bell rang, Tiffany Burgess was in Principal McNair's office.

"Thank you for coming in today, Ms. Burgess. Please take a seat." He directed Tiffany to the two seats on the other side of his desk.

Tiffany looked around nervously.

Principal McNair wanted her to feel comfortable. "You're not in trouble Ms. Burgess. This will only take a few minutes."

Tiffany chose a seat. Principal McNair explained to her that he was alarmed by seeing both of Kayla's parents two days in a row, and that he was made aware of an altercation he was sure she was aware of.

Tiffany stumbled over her words. "I don't really know what happened. I just know that Kayla yelled at Brian in the cafeteria Monday. I wasn't close to them to witness it."

"What did she say to him?"

"I don't know," Tiffany answered.

Principal McNair couldn't decide if believed her or not. "So, you know that she yelled at Brian, but you don't know why or what she said?" He wanted to make sure he clearly understood what she had said.

"Yes."

"Do you know where Kayla is now?"

"I honestly haven't talked to her since her party Saturday."

"I thought you two were best friends. You've been joined at the hip since freshman year." It wasn't that Principal McNair was interested in student drama; he just wanted to be sure that whatever was going on between Tiffany and Kayla had nothing to do with her being missing.

"We were. It's just been a weird couple of weeks," Tiffany offered Principal McNair a smirk. He studied her face.

Tiffany had always been a good student. For Kayla and Tiffany to be the most popular girls at the school, even more popular than the seniors, they were really good girls. He had never had a problem out of either of them. They were consistently on the A honor roll and apparently, their popularity got out around the city, and now other students were trying to come to Harriet Tubman High School.

Tiffany obviously wasn't going to offer Principal McNair any more information than he asked for. Her wavy, dirty blonde hair dropped a few inches below her shoulder. She began twirling it. Principal McNair had enough of the silent treatment.

"Thank you, Ms. Burgess. Grab a pass on your way back to class."

Tiffany walked out without another word. He called the counselor to request that she send in the next student. A few moments later, Brian Patterson entered his office after a faint knock. The senior's head almost brushed the doorframe. He dipped his head out of habit.

"Please take a seat, Mr. Patterson."

"What's going on, Mr. McNair?" Brian didn't waste any time.

"Kayla Carlisle is missing. Do you know where she is?"

Brian sighed. He shook his head in exasperation. He rubbed his forehead for a few seconds. He then looked up at the ceiling while tucking in his lips. He let out a long sigh. Principal McNair watched him patiently. When their eyes met again, he could tell that Brian was fighting back tears.

"No. I have no idea where she is."

"I'm told you two had an argument before she went missing."

"We did. She thinks I was – " Brian stopped mid-sentence. Principal McNair waited for him to correct himself. "She thinks that I was cheating on her, but I wasn't."

Just as Principal McNair thought. Student drama. He had to keep the line of questioning on Kayla's disappearance. "What was the last thing she said to you?"

Brian shook his head. He rubbed his hands up and down his thighs. "What didn't she say to me? I'm a loser. I'm a dog. No good. She can't believe me. It's all a blur, really. I just couldn't believe how she looked at me. She looked at me like I was the lowest scum of the earth. I think it's Jenna. We never had problems until Jenna. I swear, that girl is evil."

Principal McNair thought for a second. "Jenna?" he asked.

"That beanpole ass - oops. Sorry Mr. McNair. Uhm… the new girl."

"Oh, yes. Janice Tayler. The girl from Connecticut. She's only been here what? A month?"

"And that's a month too long."

"What exactly did Jenna do?"

"She's been in Kayla's ear, lying about me cheating. She's always been cold to me too. I don't know what she has against me, but Kayla and I never got into it about things like that until her."

"Apparently, Kayla had a party Saturday." Principal McNair wanted to keep Brian talking.

"Supposedly, that's when I got caught cheating. She swore that I was…" Brian stopped.

"That you were what?" Principal McNair wasn't one for teenage gossip, but these stories were beginning to make him suspicious.

"That I was messing around with someone else," Brian finished. Principal McNair sensed a change in Brian's demeanor.

"She stormed out of the party with Jenna. She didn't answer any of my calls. She didn't respond to any of my texts. I tried to go by her house Sunday. Her little brother told me that she wasn't there. I'm not even sure if he was telling the truth. I didn't see her again until lunch Monday. I just walked over to her to talk, and that's when she just went ballistic. She started yelling all those horrible things. The whole cafeteria was watching. I just walked out. I didn't want to be the center of attention."

"Did you see her again after that?"

"No. I was so embarrassed. I didn't even text her again until later that night. But, just like Saturday, Sunday, and Monday morning… no response. I didn't find out that she was missing until yesterday. Someone saw her mom crying in the hallway."

"Yes. Ms. Washington was here yesterday. Do you have any idea where Kayla could be?"

"I wish I did. Her dad grilled me yesterday. I don't think he ever really liked me. My mom let him in the house. He was waiting in our living room. I didn't like his tone, but I tried to stay calm. But, it was like he was accusing me of doing something. I would never hurt Kayla. We had been together for almost two years."

Principal McNair felt like Brian was trying to convince him. He knew that Brian had anger issues, but he didn't think he'd hurt Kayla. He saw the way they were together.

"I know, Mr. Patterson. Thank you for coming in."

"Is that it?" Brian asked, and Principal McNair nodded.

Brian stood, but he lingered. Principal McNair looked at him with concern.

"Please, tell me if you hear anything, Mr. McNair. Her parents are acting like I'm the enemy or something. Her friends look at me funny. It's like no one cares about my feelings. They act like I wasn't close to Kayla too. It's like they're all against me."

Principal McNair nodded to let Brian know that he understood. He wanted to stand to give Brian a handshake or maybe even embrace him with a hug, but he hated how the senior boys towered him. Especially Brian. He was the tallest student in the school. Principal McNair had to maintain his authority as much as he could.

"Take care, Mr. Patterson. Make sure you get a pass before returning to class." He waited until Brian closed his door.

He dialed the counselor again. "Who are you sending in next?" he asked her.

"Demetrius is ready to see you."

"Can you also call the new girl, Janice Tayler?"

"I've already called her. She will be in after Demetrius."

Principal McNair smiled. He was always proud that he hired the most attentive staff in the school district. They never failed to make him look good.

"Thank you. Please send Demetrius in."

A few moments later, he heard a knock at the door. "Please come in, Ms. Green."

Demetrius entered his office. She closed the door behind her and stood by it. She looked at the empty chairs in front of the principal's desk. He motioned for her to sit in one, and she sat down.

"Thank you for coming, Ms. Green. This won't take long at all. It has come to my attention that Kayla Carlisle is missing and I just wanted to talk to her friends to see if they had any information." Principal McNair knew that Demetrius was the most timid of their bunch. She always hung in the background and hardly spoke, but she was a sweet girl and an okay student. He could see her grades slowly improving. She was a making a 180 turn from the girl he saw when she first arrived.

"Oh my God, I have no idea what's going on." Demetrius immediately began bawling. Principal McNair was not prepared. Demetrius began, "I've been asking everyone what's happened. Jenna thinks she just ran away. Tiffany is sad, but she's not saying anything. Brian is being really weird. Her parents are a dead end. I don't know what to do."

Principal McNair passed Demetrius a box of tissues. "When was the last time you saw her?"

"I last saw her on Saturday morning, when we went on our weekly run. I had promised my grand mom that I would go to her 80th birthday party, so I missed Kayla's party. I saw her in the hallway Monday morning, but we didn't have a chance to talk. We don't share lunch on Mondays. I would have seen her in class Monday afternoon, but she never showed up. I didn't know she was missing until Tuesday." She sniffled in between every sentence.

Principal McNair could tell that Demetrius wasn't going to be any help. She seemed to miss each important event that led up to her disappearance.

"Do you have any idea where she could possibly be?"

"Her phone is dead. She doesn't respond to our texts. This is really scary. I'm so scared." Demetrius started crying uncontrollably.

"I understand. I'm sorry to bring this up. I want you to spend some time with the nurse before you return to class. Take a few moments to compose yourself, and we'll get you a pass when you're ready."

Demetrius wiped her face and tried to straighten up. "No, I'm fine. It's just. I'm fine." Principal McNair could tell that Demetrius tried to fight back her tears.

He called the nurse to escort Demetrius to her office. He would have normally called the counselor, but he figured she was busy with Jenna. Demetrius contested the nurse's help, but eventually followed her out. Principal McNair quickly asked the counselor to send Jenna in. He wanted to put the questioning behind him.

Jenna walked right in and sat down.

"Thank you for coming Ms. Tayler."

"This is about Kayla, isn't it?" she asked. "Everyone thinks she disappeared, but I'm pretty sure she's just taking a break. Did you know that Tiffany was messing with Brian behind her back?"

Principal McNair was stunned by the accusation as well as the fact that a student spoke to him so candidly about student gossip. Principal McNair couldn't understand how Jenna was a friend of Kayla's. She seemed so different. The only thing he saw similar between the two was long black hair.

He attempted to redirect the questioning. "When was the last time you saw Ms. Carlisle?"

"Monday at lunch. Brian was trying to give her an excuse as to why he's such a liar and a cheater. She was so upset. Can you imagine having to come to the same school with your manipulative childhood best friend and cheating high school sweetheart every single day? I probably would have needed to clear my head too."

"Do you have any idea where she could be now?"

"Principal McNair, I doubt that she'd want to tell me. After your lifelong best friend disrespects you like that, you tend not to trust anyone."

"How long have you two been friends?" Principal McNair asked a question, even though he was sure he had the answer.

"Since I got here. She sat next to me at lunch on my first day and we've been friends ever since." Jenna smiled.

Principal McNair wasn't sure what to make of Jenna or her responses. She was the only student that he didn't know much about. He remembered that her father was the one who came to register her for the school. That morning, he remembered thinking they looked more like trailer trash, but Jenna no longer looked the way she had on her first day.

He knew that the hair was a wig. Being a high school principal, he had come to know the difference between extensions and what he thought was real hair. All the girls seemed to be interested in fake hair, nails, and globs of makeup. Apparently, Jenna got with the program soon after she started.

Jenna stood. "I will let you know if she says anything, but I bet she'll be back by next week. She'll probably be refreshed and have a new look."

Still stunned by Jenna's demeanor, all Principal McNair could manage was, "Okay." Jenna left his office. He had forgotten to tell her to get pass on her way to class. He figured that she was so different because she wasn't a native. Implants to the city very seldom acted like natives, so he let it pass.

Principal McNair's questioning was last week, and he was no closer to finding out where Kayla was now than he was then. He finished an unofficial search of the school grounds with Mr. Carlisle and some volunteers that he rounded up. Detectives even brought in a search team complete with dogs to search the school. No one knew where Kayla was, but other than her mom's persistence, most people just figured she ran away. He didn't know much about Kayla, other than that she made his school look good.

Now, students were calling for some type of closure and he felt compelled to comply. He was planning a vigil at the Friday night football game. Harriet Tubman was to play their rival school, the Moorish Knights. This game was historically the biggest game of the season. The game drew so many people that it moved from the school district's stadium to the local national football stadium.

Principal McNair had invited the local press, the whole school district, and local politicians. He also tried reaching out to get representatives from the Carlisle family, but he didn't have any luck. At first, Mr. Carlisle was in constant contact with him, but since his planning of the vigil, Mr. Carlisle had become MIA. He'd hate to have the vigil without a family representative present, but it was starting to look like that's what would happen.

The students had been calling for it, so he really hoped this vigil would help settle the students in the surrounding areas and remind the news stations that they were still missing a Tubman teen, regardless of whether she ran away.

9 DOUG CARLISLE

It was the seventh call that Doug had missed from Principal McNair. It wasn't that he didn't want to be present at the vigil. It was that he knew that it would have so much coverage. It had finally dawned on him that his lifestyle was going to be dramatically affected by his daughter's disappearance, and he wasn't in a rush for it.

Theresa was literally going crazy. There was no way that he could add to the misery that she had already felt. He had wanted to tell her for years, but it was never the right time. He sat on the couch staring at the TV, although he had no idea what was on.

Wearing nothing but lingerie, Lisa slid into his lap on the couch.

"Do you want to watch that or watch me?" she asked him. Doug always came home on Wednesday, and Lisa had some type of surprise for him. Normally, it was what he looked forward to, but now with Kayla missing, nothing excited him anymore. He knew that he had failed her as a father. He constantly considered alternative decisions that he should have made throughout his life, decisions that would not result in Kayla running away. He knew why she left. He knew it was all his fault.

Reading Doug's expression, Lisa's face turned from excitement to concern. "What's wrong, sweetheart?"

"Nothing, I'm fine," he spoke.

Lisa started kissing his neck. Her long hair tickled his arm. She whispered in his ear, "I know how to make you feel better."

She began kissing his face. He pushed her away. "Not now, please. I just have a lot of my mind. I need to think."

"Okay," Lisa said disappointed. She slid next to him on the couch and she began massaging his neck with her hand.

He wished her gentle touch was enough to take away all of his pain. Her gentle touch, accommodating personality and insatiable desire to please him were what made him propose six years ago. It didn't hurt that she had a perfect body and flawless face to match. The relationship was so exciting and moved so fast that the wedding came only two months after the proposal, and their son was born nine months after that. Life was perfect with her. That family was perfect.

His family with Theresa was stress on top of problem on top of dismay. He wanted to leave her so many times, but he never did. He knew how much she loved him, which is what made him stay around. He thought if a woman loved him that much, what was the harm in being available?

He wanted to leave eighteen years ago, but she became pregnant with Kayla. They went back and forth for years. He had even managed to escape her once, but she refused to let him see his daughter. He figured it wasn't a big deal to play to her good graces if it meant unlimited time with his daughter. Every time they would argue, it would make Kayla cry. He never wanted to be the man to break her heart, so he built the façade of a perfect family in front of her. Being away from Theresa for stretches at a time helped him grin and bear any frustration she would bring him.

Doug looked over at Lisa who was still rubbing his neck. "Thank you, baby. You know I love you, right?" He kissed her on her cheek.

"I know," she smiled.

"Where's Junior?"

"You know he's sleeping."

Doug's phone buzzed. Lisa reached to hand it to him with her left hand, and without missing a beat continued to massage his neck with her right hand. Doug looked at the phone. It was a text message from Principal McNair.

We're going to honor Kayla at this Friday's game. We'd love to have a family member there, but we understand if it's too painful for you to attend. We just want the whole city to know how much she meant to us. Hopefully the coverage will help us reach her. Thank you. I'm available if you need me.

Doug blinked away his tears as he read the text message. Doug bitched to everyone who would listen about how Kayla's story was being dismantled. The news made it seem like she was an oversexed teenager. They left out her great personality and grades. Her friends couldn't agree on what they thought happened to her, but these were the people she spent so much time with. Rumors were all over the city about her being a drug addict and a slut. Everyone wanted a juicy story but didn't want to remember the good-hearted person that his daughter was. That his daughter is.

Doug knew this vigil was Principal McNair's way of drawing positive attention to Kayla. He really should be there, but it was likely that the story would be all over the news. It wasn't just that his common-law wife and real wife would find out, but so would their family and friends.

He could never forget how devastated Kayla was when she found out about Lisa. She had just started high school at Harriet Tubman. Wednesday through Saturday was always his time to spend with Lisa and Junior. Doug didn't know it, but Kayla was spending that Saturday with her best friend and somehow they ended up at the mall across town. The same mall where Doug took Lisa to shop every other weekend.

Doug was so tired of shopping that he begged Lisa for a break. They went to the food court and found a large table that could handle them and their group of bags. Junior was asleep in the small stroller beside them. Doug couldn't remember what they were eating that day, but he knew he was glowing, and so was Lisa. They were always such a perfect couple. Their number was called, so Doug went to grab their food to bring it to their table. As soon as he looked up, he saw his daughter staring at him through red-rimmed eyes. He had no clue how long she had been watching him.

Apparently, Kayla was shopping with Tiffany and her mom in a nearby store when she saw him. She excused herself from the store to confront him but turned into a frozen statue. Her white T-shirt was wet from the tears streaming down her crumpled face. His heart sank as he watched the innocence leave his little girl. That would be the last time he'd see her signature double braided hair, basketball shorts and tennis shoes. Doug was sure that the only tennis shoes Kayla now owned were cheer shoes.

"Baby, are you listening to me?" He heard Lisa ask.

"Huh?" he turned to look at her.

"Do you know that little girl? She has the same last name as us."

Doug followed Lisa's gaze to the TV. The screen was covered with the last image he had seen of his only daughter. He gave her a forehead kiss right after she took that picture and right before she left for school. He felt his eyes begin to well up.

"I need to use the restroom," he said as he left the couch.

"She's so pretty. I hope they find her," he heard Lisa say.

As soon as Doug closed the bathroom door, the tears began to flow. He locked the door to make sure Lisa didn't walk in on him. He didn't feel like explaining himself, although he knew he needed to.

He couldn't help but to wonder what type of girl Kayla would be if it wasn't for his double life. He made a horrible agreement with her after she found out. All he could think of was that he wanted to wipe away his daughter's tears, but not mess up his life with his wife. In exchange for silence, Kayla was showered with her new lifestyle. Her no-restriction credit card purchases included new clothes, hair, nails, and makeup. Every week that he saw Kayla, she was turning into someone he didn't know, but there was nothing he could say.

He couldn't deny that his daughter looked like a model. She was flawless, something any man would be attracted to, and he hated it. He would talk to her everyday about her innocence, about keeping her virginity and how she was smarter than just looks. Theresa didn't like it at first, but it seemed that Kayla was happy and she knew how close Doug was with his daughter. She didn't want to do anything to destroy their relationship. Kayla maintained the A honor roll and never got in trouble. They didn't see any harm in her new lifestyle.

Often when they were alone, Kayla would ask Doug why. No matter how many times he answered, the question was always the same. It was the same Sunday night after dinner, the night before her disappearance. He could remember the conversation like it was yesterday.

He walked into Kayla's room to talk to her, like he did most nights he was there. He'd always talk to Junior, then talk to Kayla. He caught her removing shades from her face and wiping her eyes but wasn't sure if she was crying. She cried for weeks after she found out he led a double life, but he never saw her like that again.

"Are you okay?" he asked.

"I'm fine, Doug," she said flatly. She stopped calling him dad after she found out about Lisa. He hated it but tolerated it, just like he tolerated her mother.

"How's Lisa?" she asked as if she was genuinely concerned, but Doug was familiar with the song and dance.

"She's fine," he simply answered.

"You know, I've been wondering. If you guys have a daughter, does that mean you will replace me?"

That hurt him. He closed her door, then walked toward her to give her a hug. She walked around him and sat on the bed. She was more nonchalant than usual. Doug didn't know if he was reading her correctly, but always approached her with patience.

"It's crazy how fast men can replace women. I used to think maybe beauty would work, but I'm convinced it doesn't matter what a girl does. Men will do what they want, when they want, and with whom they want. What if girls did the same?"

He didn't like the tone in her voice. Her words seemed so apathetic.

"Did something happen between you and Brian?" he asked cautiously. He hated Brian from the first moment he met him. He knew Kayla dated the boy to spite him but thought it would be a phase. Two years later, and they were still an item. Doug knew Brian's type. He was just like him. He was the star football player that all the girls wanted, with a temper that could surprise a fly. The boy could have a girl for each day of the week, and he chose to date his daughter.

Kayla rolled her head toward her dad. She gave a mischievous smile. "You would love that now wouldn't you?"

"Hell no! Kayla, why would you say that?" He didn't even try to understand her line of questioning anymore. He had been walking on eggshells with her for two years and was now feeling like he was losing her more than he had before.

"Well you have nothing to worry about. I'm done with Brian and Tiffany. I'm done with everyone who lies to me." She gave a lingering look at her dad. He was stuck. He couldn't think of anything to say. Kayla rolled over onto her bed and scrolled through her social media timelines.

Doug sighed. He looked around the room at the expensive furniture, the custom-built shoe wall full of high heels. He stepped onto the plush rug that lay next to Kayla's bed to sit on the bed next to her. He thought about all those years he worked busting his ass to build a profitable company so he could work from anywhere. All he had to do was review daily reports and make sure his systems ran smoothly. His workers did all the real work. He built the perfect excuse for his life, telling his wives that he worked for a trucking company alternating his work days. Everything he did was to please the women in his life, but now the most important one couldn't even look at him. She didn't even respect him.

"I know I've made a lot of mistakes, and I really want to make it right. I'm sorry."

Kayla didn't respond. She lay on her back, held her phone toward the ceiling, and narrowed her eyes. Another selfie. Doug remembered thinking that all she did was take selfies. Doug knew through all of the smiling pictures and new friends that Kayla truly wasn't happy. He knew it because she kept the same look in her eyes that he had. He had burdened her with lying to her mother and brother, all for the façade of happiness. He showered Lisa and Kayla with things he thought would make them happy and spoiled Theresa with scheduled undivided attention. Theresa was never a money hungry woman.

He touched Kayla's shoulder. She turned to face him. Her eyes looked empty. "I understand, Doug. I've been making a lot of mistakes too, and I'm going to make it right."

"What does that mean?" Doug asked her.

"Mommy made your favorite meal. You know… before you go off to be with your favorite family." Kayla rolled off the other side of the bed.

Doug stood. Her words were becoming colder and colder. "Baby girl," he started.

She turned right before reaching her door. "Doug, just stay with them. Mommy may tolerate it, but I can't stand it. I can't stand sorry men. I'd rather be around honest bums than a lying family who claims that they love me." Kayla left the room before Doug could respond.

She didn't speak with him the rest of the night. She smiled and joked with her mom and brother, took a picture of her food to post online and faked happy like she had always done. She had become so good at it that Doug could no longer tell her true feelings.

"Sweetheart. Are you okay?" Lisa knocked on the bathroom door.

He sucked up his sobs and deepened his voice. "Yea baby, just constipated. I'll be in here for a while."

"Eww," she teased. "Take a shower before you come to bed. I'll be there waiting."

He thought back to Kayla telling him goodbye that morning as she always had; he kissed her on her forehead like he had always done as well. It was like the night before had never happened. That was the last time he saw his daughter; continuing to live the lie of a perfect, fairytale family.

When he heard that she was missing, he figured that she was trying to prove a point. He drilled her friends for information on her whereabouts. Was she cunning enough to fool even them? He decided that if she could be convincing to her dad, then she could be convincing to her friends.

Theresa was sure that Kayla was in danger, so Doug made sure to thoroughly search for her. He even got help from his friends to continue the search in his absence. He didn't want her to lie dead in a ditch nearby while he was thinking she had run away, but the lack of evidence assured him that she had left; that and the fact that he kept replaying her last words to him over and over in his head.

Doug knew that being popular and having good grades weren't enough to fake her happiness. Just like he knew that his money and perfect family wasn't enough to fake his - especially with his baby girl missing. She had to know that he wanted to make it right with her. He had given her enough space. A week and a half was enough.

Doug texted Principal McNair that he would be there on Friday on behalf of the family. He had enough of putting his women above his baby girl. They'd have to find out sooner or later, and what better time than now? Especially if he thought it gave him a chance at seeing his daughter again.

10 TASHA

Tasha had enough of Kayla. When she was at school it was all about her. Her new cheer routine. Her joining the National Junior Honor Society. Her dating the superstar athlete - the same superstar athlete that was interested in Tasha before he had ever seen a Kayla. Now that Kayla had been gone for almost two weeks, she still had to endure an entire ceremony dedicated to Kayla.

Tasha had always looked forward to the Tubman vs Moors football game, but she was actually considering skipping it this year.

"Come on, Tasha. It's one little ceremony during halftime. You are such a hater," Tasha's friend, Jo, pleaded with her.

"You don't think it's a little obsessive? Can I get one day without hearing about Kayla? You know she wasn't the saint people made her out to be."

Jo looked at Tasha in disbelief. "Girl, boo."

"She was a damn junkie. At her party, I heard the DJ say she was one of White Boy Steve's biggest customers."

"So, you checking for her now?"

"I just noticed is all."

"The whole school district gets their Adderall from White Boy Steve. So? You pop 'em too. Does that make you a junkie now?"

"Naw. I told you she was on more than just Adderall."

"She gone, Tasha. Leave it alone. Now come to the game tomorrow. I got a new outfit and everything. Don't tell me that you didn't get a fit."

"I got something the wear." Tasha decided to stop pressing the issue. She didn't want to seem like a hater, but Kayla seriously wasn't all that.

Tasha still remembered Kayla from middle school, back when she wore basketball shorts, T-shirts, and name brand tennis shoes every day. Tasha was a little jealous then because her mom couldn't afford the expensive tennis shoes, but that wasn't why Tasha didn't like her. Kayla was a mean girl.

Tasha was late for the first time ever to Ms. Jacob's 6th grade class. Her seat was in the front of the class, closest to the teacher's desk. It was a rough morning. Her mom's car had broken down again and she had to flag her neighbors down until she found one who could drop her off at school. When Tasha finally made it into class and rushed to her seat near Ms. Jacobs, she was devastated when she saw that it was occupied. A new student was sitting there.

Tasha felt like she was well within her right. She walked up to her seat occupied by the girl she now knew as Kayla. "This is my seat. You need to find another one," she said to Kayla.

Kayla just looked at her. Where Tasha was from, looks could start a fight faster than any words could. She leaned toward Kayla's face to give her a piece of her mind when she heard Ms. Jacob call to her.

"Tasha, you're already late. Please take a seat in the back."

"But, I've been sitting here the whole six weeks. Where'd this girl come from?" She talked about Kayla like she wasn't there.

"Mind your manners, Tasha. Be the example. Please, take the seat in the back."

Tasha whispered into Kayla's ear, "This isn't over, bitch."

Tasha had talked up a fight all day, telling anyone who would listen that she was going to beat that new bitch's ass, and the school was hype. The whole school made sure Kayla and Tasha's whereabouts were known at all times, so that the fight would surely happen. It had been a long time since there was excitement at Nat Turner Middle School, and this fight was scheduled to be the event of the year.

Tasha was looking forward to proving to the entire school that she wasn't to be messed with. She couldn't even focus in class because she thought over and over how she was going to make the new girl the laughing stock of middle school.

The end of the day school bell had finally rung. Tasha was immediately reminded about the fight and told of Kayla's whereabouts. She walked up to Kayla as soon as she walked out of the school building. Tasha swallowed her nerves, as she had always done before a fight. Her greatest skill was the surprise blow to the head that she usually gave her victims. Before they realized what hit them, she'd follow with a few more and have the fight won before it had ever really started. Usually, an adult would be near enough to break it up by then.

She ran up to Kayla and leaned into a punch to sting her left eye, but to her surprise, Kayla weaved the blow. Tasha hurled over, clutching her stomach. It all happened so fast that she didn't realize Kayla engraved her midsection with her fist. Astonished, she looked up at Kayla, who stood determined in a fighting stance, waiting for Tasha's next move.

Tasha couldn't believe it. Kayla's perfectly braided hair, wrinkle free shirt, and brand-new shoes looked like that of a Foot Locker model, not a fighter. She looked around to see if anyone noticed. "Come on Tasha. Are you just going to take that?" a student yelled at her. She couldn't even see if there were teachers near because the students clouded every angle.

"Principal's office," Ms. Smith called as she emerged through the crowd. She held both girls by the arm and dragged them along with her. Tasha hoped it didn't show, but she was grateful for the save.

The fight could have ended worse and destroyed her reputation. This, she thought, she could recover from.

After that day, she swore up and down that Ms. Smith saved Kayla from the beat-down of her life. Most of the kids had seen Tasha fight before, so no one really doubted her skills. She told them that the principal made her promise not to fight Kayla or she'd get kicked out of the school, but that was far from the truth. The principal was going to suspend both of them, but Kayla interjected. It was the first time Tasha had heard Kayla speak.

"I'm sorry about all this," Kayla pled. "It was just a misunderstanding. We're good now. It will never be an issue again."

Tasha agreed, but only after the principal asked her. Tasha never made eye contact with Kayla.

A few weeks passed, and Tasha was finally thinking of releasing her hate of Kayla. She walked up behind her as she talked with Pretty Girl Tiffany. That's what everyone called Tiffany because she had long hair, long legs, and long nails. She looked like a true model without even trying; the epitome of pretty to middle schoolers. She had overheard Tiffany asking Kayla about Tasha.

"I saw that fight. You could have beat her up easily. Maybe then she wouldn't be such a bully," Tiffany said to Kayla.

"My dad taught me about people like that. They pick fights because they don't have anything else going for themselves. As long as she doesn't bother me, I really don't care to prove that I can beat her up. I already know that I can."

That was it. Tasha had no reason to be her friend. She talked behind
her back and spread rumors that she had nothing going for herself.
Kayla didn't even know Tasha. How would she know what she had
going for herself? Tasha knew right then what type of girl Kayla was.
A manipulator and a back stabber. She wore new, name brand
clothes every day and wanted to be the center of attention. She even
manipulated her way into becoming best friends with Pretty Girl
Tiffany.

Tasha didn't want to be anywhere near Kayla at that point. She knew
that she must have been a snake. That's why it didn't surprise Tasha
when she caught Kayla cheating on tests, when she kissed Eric that
time in the back of the cafeteria, when she started dressing like a slut
in high school, or when she saw her sniffing coke in the bathroom
last week.

She had been wanting to tell people that Kayla wasn't an angel all
these years, but somehow everyone was under her spell. Everyone
thought she was some dynamic diva or Ms. Perfect. Even her best
friend, Jo, would call her a Kayla hater if she said anything bad about
her, which is why after all those years, she kept her secrets silent.
That was, until she found out something big enough to tell everyone.

Last Monday, Tasha had walked into the restroom after lunch. She
heard someone sniffing something, but didn't think anything of it.
That was until she saw Kayla walk out of the stall wiping powder
away from her nose. Tasha acted like she didn't see it and walked

into the next stall. She didn't exit until she heard Kayla leave. Tasha couldn't wait to tell Jo what she had seen, but soon as she made it to class, everyone was talking about the fight that Kayla had in the lunchroom with Brian. Tasha smirked, *Perfect couple huh,* she thought to herself. She didn't want to seem too eager, so she decided to casually tell Jo in the Tuesday morning class that they shared together, but by Tuesday, word had gotten out that Kayla might have run away.

"She must have left after doing those coke lines," Tasha said jokingly to Jo after she heard the news.

"What?" Jo asked her in disbelief.

"I saw her in the bathroom after lunch."

"Really? Doing coke on the counters? No one does that. Not out in the open where everyone can see."

"No, not on the counters. I saw her wiping her nose when she came out of the stall."

"Cut it out, Tasha. I'm sure she was crying after what happened with her and Brian. Her nose was probably running. You're always trying to make her out to be a villain. Besides, how many coke heads do we know in this class?" Jo whispered. She was referring to the McAlister twins. Those two talked about their habit like it was having lunch.

"I'm just saying." Tasha decided that she wouldn't refer to Kayla anymore. Jo was starting to get on her nerves making her out to be a hater.

Now that there were still no signs of Kayla, Tasha thought she had finally gotten rid of her archenemy until day in and day out, rumors begin to surface about Kayla's whereabouts. And now, there was this memorial. They acted like the girl was dead. Tasha didn't wish her dead, but she did enjoy the thought of going another day without hearing her name.

Tasha scrolled down the pictures in her phone to find the selfie she took in the mirror of the outfit she had bought over the weekend. Every week she got paid, she bought a new outfit. She didn't want to relive her middle school days of old hand me downs. She finally found the picture she was looking for. It was her trying on her new jumper.

"I'll probably wear this." She shoved the phone into Jo's face.

"Ooh girl, when did you get that?" Jo asked. "You always got a fresh new fit."

Tasha smiled. She loved when people talked about how nice her clothes were, or how good she looked in something new. So what if there would be a memorial for Kayla? It's not like people would gawk at her on the sidelines this week.

"You know what?" Tasha added. "I was thinking about getting my hair cut this weekend too." She was going to make it her mission to be the center of attention at the big game Friday.

11 BRIAN

Brian knew better. He knew he should have sat that game out, but he didn't. It was the game of the season. His last season. All of the college football scouts were there. He winced, remembering when he and Kayla had planned to wear matching temporary face tattoos for the game. The sudden thought made him want to cry.

"Man, I told y'all to keep Brian out of the game. It's all his fault that we lost."

Brian looked up at the sound of his name. It was Eric. The wide receiver who could hardly catch, but always found fault in Brian's decisions on the field.

"So are we going to forget those three passes you missed?" Brian barked. He ran up to Eric, ready to weld his head into the lockers behind them.

"Come on, guys." A few players jumped between them. Everyone knew that Brian had a temper and wouldn't back down from a fight.

"Man, you played like shit last week and played even worse this week. Everyone knows it. Get your head in the game or get off the field," Eric scolded.

Brian thought that if he could just get to him, he'd make him eat those words. He'd been waiting for a reason to make an example of Eric. He still hadn't forgotten when Eric tried to come onto Kayla even after she told him that she was dating Brian.

"Brian. I need to see you now," Coach called.

Brian left the near scuffle to meet with his coach, but not before casting a lingering scowl toward Eric. The team waited until Coach gained Brian's full attention before leaving Eric's side.

"Brian, I know it's been a rough couple of weeks for you. I want you to go ahead and head out. Coach D is going to escort you out the back."

Brian didn't know if he was supposed to feel regret or relief. Coach normally chewed him out for any mistake he'd make, but he hadn't said much to him since the school found out about Kayla's disappearance.

"I'm fine, Coach."

"I know you're playing the tough guy right now, but you don't need to. Besides, we have way too much press here tonight who'd love to shove a camera in your face. That's too much pressure for anyone to deal with. Follow Coach D out now. I'm going to stall the press." Coach walked away, while Coach D motioned for Brian to follow him out.

"I need to meet up with my mom, Coach," Brian said to Coach D.

"She's waiting out here for you son."

Just as Coach D said, his mom was in the parking lot waiting for him. She was in the driver's side of his red Dodge Charger with the engine idling. She offered him a weak smile when he got inside.

"It's gon' be alright, baby," she said as she began to drive off.

Brian's phone rang. He looked and saw that it was his friend, Jason, calling. He stared at it, trying to decide if he should answer or not.

"Why don't you give your phone a break for a while, son," his mom said. He thought maybe she was right. He had been attached to his phone, hoping for a response from Kayla since she left him after her party. He silenced his ringer. They rode in silence the entire trip home.

Maybe it was time Brian realized that Kayla wasn't coming back. He first thought it was just a cruel joke that she was playing on him. He couldn't blame her for thinking that he had slept with Tiffany. She did find him in the room with her and Tiffany was completely naked. He thought over and over about that night and was no closer to any answers.

Brian began planning the surprise party as soon as he knew that his mom would be away on business that weekend, but it was Tiffany's idea to buy Kayla the $1000.00 pair of high end, high heeled shoes that she wanted. Almost every week, Kayla would post a #shoeporn picture on her page. Tiffany knew that she would love them. Brian only agreed because he knew how much she loved the shoe and that he couldn't afford them on his own. He definitely didn't want her best friend to upstage him. The surprise party was the perfect place to reveal the gift.

It was just about time for him and Tiffany to bring out the shoes. He looked around the party for Tiffany but couldn't find her. Brian had finally decided that he'd go ahead and grab the shoes from his room, where they had hidden them. When he walked inside of his room, Tiffany was lying naked on his bed. The room was dark, except for the dim lamp lit in the corner.

"What are you doing?" he asked Tiffany.

Tiffany sat up on the bed. She looked drowsy. Her eyes were really low, and the corner of her lips were curled. "Sleeping," she said, although it sounded more like a question.

"Where are your clothes?"

Tiffany motioned toward Brian's desk while falling back onto the bed. He followed her finger to find her clothes. He grabbed the neatly folded clothes from the desk and sat on the bed next to Tiffany.

"Put your clothes back on. You can't let Kayla see you like this."

Tiffany didn't seem to be responding. It appeared to Brian that she had fallen asleep. He figured it was best to get her dressed and figure out the rest later. He fumbled with her panties, trying to figure out which side went where. He managed to get them around her ankles and proceeded to pull them up her legs when his door slid open.

It was Jenna, followed by Kayla. The smiles they wore faded quickly. Jenna wore a look of surprise while Kayla's was one of disgust. He dropped Tiffany's legs. He looked at Tiffany's completely naked body lying next to him on his bed, then back at Kayla. Tears streamed down her face.

"What's going on?" he heard Tiffany say. He looked back at Tiffany, who sat up looking at Jenna and Kayla. "Oh, hey guys," she slurred. She fell back onto the bed. *Something just isn't right*, Brian thought to himself.

"Let's go," Jenna said to Kayla as she turned to usher her out of the doorway. She closed the door behind her.

Brian left Tiffany lying on his bed with her panties around her ankle. He ran to follow Kayla. She was getting into the passenger side of Jenna's car.

"Kayla, something is wrong with Tiffany." Brian grabbed the car door before she closed it.

"Looks like you two are getting along fine!" Kayla yelled at him.

"I told you," Jenna said. "It sucks that I'm right, but I knew it was something between them two. He doesn't deserve you. Let's get out of here."

Kayla struggled to get the door from Brian.

"She's lying, Kayla. There's nothing going on between us. I swear. I found her in my room like that."

Kayla let go of the door and covered her face. She couldn't stop crying.

"Get away from us!" Jenna yelled louder than necessary. Brian saw that people were starting to notice them. They were looking at him with concern. It was rumored that he had anger issues, so he already knew what the scene may have looked like to them. A skinny little white girl running scared from a 6'4" stark black athlete. He let go of the door, and Jenna's tires screeched.

He ran back to his room to get answers from Tiffany, but when he opened his bedroom door, he realized that she was fast asleep. He thought it was best to leave her there. He dialed Kayla's phone over and over again, but there was no answer. He sent endless texts with no responses.

Brian's mom finally pulled into their driveway. He saw that he had missed ten more calls in their route home. Neither of them was from Kayla, so he ignored them. Still, no messages from her either.

"Are you hungry?" his mom asked as they walked into the house.

"No. I'm just going to go to bed."

Other than class and football practice, Brian did nothing else. He didn't even realize that he loved Kayla so much until she disappeared. Or, maybe it was how she disappeared. He had so many questions and no answers. Jenna swore he was a liar and a cheater. Tiffany wouldn't even look at him, let alone respond to his texts. Demetrius seemed as lost as she always did. Kayla's parents treated him like a suspect, and the police lost interest in him once his alibi checked out.

He and Kayla were a great couple. Sure, he cheated on her when they first started dating, but it was just because she wasn't having sex. That was all he thought he cared about back then. He just didn't want to break up with her because she was becoming a local celebrity. People thought they were the perfect power couple. Who was he to break up their image?

After a year of dating, he realized that she was becoming his best friend. She inspired him. She had dreams and goals outside of him, but still had room for him. He didn't see it coming, but he really fell for her. He had finally gotten used to life without sex, until Kayla hit him with a surprise.

She told him for her birthday, she wanted to lose her virginity. He hadn't mentioned sex in months, so he was confused about why she brought it up, but he wasn't going to mess up the mood. They planned it perfectly, and it happened just as they planned. They'd skip their last class on her birthday and go to his house before his mom came home. It was weird, but it happened.

Kayla took a few minutes to freshen up in his bathroom. She walked slowly toward him, wearing fancy lingerie. Brian was really excited that she had gone out of her way to make the occasion special. Then, he thought maybe this was her gift to herself. He began to help Kayla get undressed, but she didn't let him. She preferred to do it herself. She even undressed him. She became more aggressive and started acted jittery, which alarmed him.

"Are you okay, Kayla?" he asked. "Are you sure you want to do this?"

"Shut up Brian. It's my birthday."

Everything was awkward after that. Kayla tried to put a sock in his mouth. She wanted to try all these things that she must have seen on a porno. Brian wanted to think that she had been lying to him and it probably wasn't her first time, but he felt it was much more than that.

Thirty minutes later, they were both dressed, preparing to go back to school. Kayla was moving a mile a minute. He didn't want to ask her but felt that he needed to. "Are you high?"

Kayla looked at him like she was offended. "Ugh. Just take me back to school, Brian."

They didn't talk about it again. Everything seemed to go back to normal. They were lovey dovey in the hallway on Thursday, they hung out after the game on Friday and then things got ugly after the surprise party on Saturday. Brian just couldn't figure out what he had done wrong, what he could have done differently.

His coaches had told him before that he needed to focus on football. It was his ticket to college. Girls come and go. Maybe this was Kayla leaving him. Their perfect tenure was over. It was time he focused back on football. If he continued to play the way he did at the big game, he'd lose more than just Kayla. He'd lose football too. He needed to get out of his head and get out of the house. He returned Jason's call.

12 MRS. JACOBS

A teacher never really knows if they're inquiring about a student's life too much or not enough, or at least that's what Mrs. Jacobs thought as she made it home from the big game. It had been odd at cheer practice since Kayla's disappearance, but to have an entire half-time show dedicated to her made it even more eerie. Since her disappearance, Mrs. Jacobs thought over and over about her relationship with Kayla. She glanced back at the text feed that she had with her.

It's my birthday, pleeease????

🙏 *I promise to be on time for practice.*

Okay. I'll see you at practice.

Mrs. Jacobs didn't think letting Kayla skip class was a bad idea. Kayla had the highest grade of all her students. She knew that Kayla was spending time with her boyfriend Brian, and she was on time for practice just as she had promised. She even seemed more perky than normal.

"How'd it go?" Mr. Jacobs asked when he walked into the living room, breaking Mrs. Jacobs of her thoughts.

"I still can't believe she just ran away like that. It doesn't really seem like her."

Mr. Jacobs knew exactly who she was talking about. She'd been talking about her missing student all week. "You said it yourself, hon. You never know what's going on with those teenagers."

When Mrs. Jacobs discussed Kayla with her husband before, he deduced Kayla's disappearance to be the result of a common behavioral change. She was starting to think that he was right. The girl seemed almost perfect. She must've gotten tired of being everything to everyone.

"I just feel like maybe I should have talked to her more. It always seems like the class clowns take up all my time. Maybe I should have asked her how she really felt at home and at school. You know, maybe she was under a lot of pressure."

"Your job was to teach her English and to teach her to cheer. Nothing else."

Mrs. Jacobs knew better than to protest with her husband about her students. He wasn't a teacher. He didn't understand that teaching was almost like being a second parent. Every year, she gained almost 100 new students and even though the old ones eventually graduated, they always came back around. She constantly wondered how they were and if she helped contribute to their successes or failures.

She looked back at her text feed again. The last text from Kayla was a picture of the temporary tattoos she received in the mail for the big game. It was sent the morning that Kayla went missing. As cheer captain, Kayla made it her personal mission to get the school excited about the games. It didn't matter if it was a big game or a regular game. Kayla thought the cheer squad was the spirit of Harriet Tubman High. Mrs. Jacobs smiled at that thought of Kayla. Kayla was trying to get things back to normal with her and Mrs. Jacobs.

"With no signs of the missing teen, Harriet Tubman High planned a vigil for Kayla Carlisle."

Mr. Jacobs turned on the television. He reached for the remote to change the channel, until he saw that Mrs. Jacobs turned to watch it.

"The police believe that she's a runaway. We don't know where she is. We just want to know that she's all right. Please Kayla, if you're watching, just let us know that you're okay."

Mrs. Jacobs watched as Kayla's dad pled into the camera. She lost interest in the television when the next news story appeared. Mr. Jacobs saw that as his chance to change the channel.

"Do you want to watch a movie dear?" he asked.

"No. I think I'll go ahead and get some rest," Mrs. Jacobs replied.

She carried her bags back to her room. She set her purse on her dresser to look into its back pocket. She saw the small vial of cocaine that she had confiscated from Kayla the Friday after her birthday. She thought over and over about giving it to police as evidence but didn't want to tarnish Kayla's image any further. She doubted if Kayla had ever even done the drug before.

After class that Friday afternoon, Kayla stopped to show Mrs. Jacobs a picture of the temporary tattoos that she had ordered. She'd only ordered enough for the cheer squad but thought that if the students liked them, the squad could use the tattoos as a fundraiser.

"I already ordered them. They should be here this weekend. I thought I had saved the picture in my phone. It shouldn't take but a minute to find it, though," Kayla said. Not paying attention, she set her bag on Mrs. Jacobs desk while still thumbing through her phone.

Her bag had only sat halfway on the desk and fell as soon as she let go of the handle. The contents of the bag spilled onto the ground, but the most noticeable item was the vial slowly rolling across the floor. Kayla looked up when she heard the vial rolling, right in time to see Mrs. Jacobs bend down to pick it up.

Mrs. Jacobs was stunned. She knew what the item was as soon as it fell out of the bag. She was aware that some of the students dabbled in coke. Some teachers did as well. Even she did if the occasion was appropriate, but she didn't expect it from Kayla. Sure, she knew Kayla would take an Adderall pill here and there to focus, as a lot of the students would, but not something as serious as cocaine.

Kayla rushed to put her things into her bag while Mrs. Jacobs stared at her. She had no clue what to say.

"It's not mine, Mrs. Jacobs," Kayla stood as she began to explain. "A friend asked me to hold it." Kayla shifted from foot to foot, holding her disheveled bag loosely in her hand.

"You know, I should turn this in." It was the only thing Mrs. Jacobs could think to say. She knew people who seemed perfectly normal on the drug, but she knew lots more who were not. She didn't think it was a gamble that Kayla should take, not when she had so much going for herself.

"Please don't, Mrs. Jacobs. I promise nothing like this will happen again." Kayla's eyes welled with tears.

"Are you using?" Mrs. Jacobs thought to how Kayla's last few assignments weren't the same quality of work as normal, but she excused it because she knew what Kayla was capable of.

"No. Never. I promise, I was just holding it for a friend."

"Sounds like you need better friends Kayla. I expect more from you." Mrs. Jacobs felt hurt. She had always thought of Kayla and her friend Tiffany as the perfect daughters she never had. Pretty, kind and smart.

"It's not me, Mrs. Jacobs. I promise I will do better."

Mrs. Jacobs sighed. "Okay, Kayla. I won't turn you in this time, but I never want to see or hear anything like this again. These aren't the mistakes you want to start making. You have a bright future ahead of you. Don't let things like this get in your way." Mrs. Jacobs was too nervous to learn any more about Kayla and the drugs; she only wanted Kayla to promise that she wouldn't do them.

"Thank you so much, Mrs. Jacobs." Kayla rushed her arms around Mrs. Jacobs. Mrs. Jacobs imagined the embrace would be the same if she had her own daughter. "I promise I won't let you down," Kayla said.

"Okay. Get out of here. We have practice soon."

Kayla rushed out of the class. Mrs. Jacobs put the vial in the back of her purse. She had almost forgotten about it, until Kayla came up missing.

Garvey Morning News took days to pick up the story. As soon as they had, they painted Kayla as a promiscuous teen from the selective pictures they gathered from her Instagram page. They caught wind of the fight she had with her boyfriend and listed her as a runaway before detectives were assigned the case. Mrs. Jacobs knew that the small vial of cocaine would really blow Kayla's story out of perspective, but could it have saved her?

Mrs. Jacobs had no idea. She didn't know if she made a good or bad decision. Of course, after almost two weeks, it was too late to tell anyone anything about it. She often thought that if Kayla was her daughter and another teacher had found the vial, she would want it to remain a secret too; that maybe she needed to stay out of the business of parents and police, and let the professionals worry about Kayla's disappearance and her image.

Principal McNair would remind the teachers often not to get into student gossip, but Mrs. Jacobs really wanted to know what Kayla's friends would say. From what she overheard from the students, Kayla and Tiffany were no longer friends and Kayla was upset with her boyfriend Brian. Neither Brian nor Tiffany had been talking to anyone much since Kayla's disappearance. She didn't know if that meant that they were guilty or that they seemed to be taking the disappearance the worst.

In the staff meeting that afternoon, Principal McNair announced that he had talked with each of Kayla's friends, the family, and the detectives, and that they were almost certain Kayla had runaway. That and the vigil had given Mrs. Jacobs some comfort, but she really wished Kayla would at least let everyone know that she was fine.

13 TIFFANY

"Come on, Tiffany. I don't have anyone to run with," Demetrius pled.

"You know that I've never really liked running. Besides, I like to sleep in on Saturdays."

"Please."

"I'll think about it. Let me get to class." Tiffany knew she wasn't getting up early to run with Demetrius on that Saturday or the next. She just told her that to get rid of her. She had been asking since the big game the Friday before.

Demetrius was trying to get Tiffany back into the friend zone, but Tiffany just wasn't up to it. All Tiffany wanted was a chance to talk to Kayla to clear things up, but it looked like she would never get that chance.

Tiffany and Brian took months to save all that money for a pair of stupid shoes. Shoes that Kayla never even had a chance to see. Word was getting around the school that Brian had raped Tiffany, but she knew it couldn't have been true. She didn't feel like she was raped, and why would Brian do such a thing? All she remembered was waking up in Brian's room Sunday morning without any clothes on.

Tiffany hated the way she felt when she had awakened. It was the same way she felt each time she thought about it. She was scared, nervous, and ashamed. How did she end up in her best friend's boyfriend's room with no clothes on?

Tiffany found her underwear barely around her ankle and saw her clothes folded on the bed next to her. She dressed in record timing and ran out of the room. She found Brian lying on the couch with a bottle of liquor dangling from his hand. He was asleep. She looked around the room, but no one else was there. She had no clue what had happened. She stood there a few moments, trying to decide if she should awaken Brian or leave him sleep. She didn't even know where her purse was.

She looked around the living room, then back into Brian's bedroom, searching for her purse. Just when she was about to give up and awaken Brian, she noticed her purse strap dangling from behind the couch. She attempted to reach over Brian to grab the purse. Brian had awakened at the wrong time. His stir to stand caused Tiffany to trip and land right on top of him.

"Get off of me!" Brian yelled. He sat up and pushed Tiffany hard. She fell on the floor. "It's all your fault," Brian's words slurred.

Tiffany was shocked. She had no idea what was going on, but she wanted to get out of there fast. Brian stood. Tiffany leapt to her feet. He gave her the same face she'd seen him give his victims. She was too familiar with Brian's anger and didn't want to be on that side of it. She had only seen him that angry on the football field, right before he punched a player from the other team. The player ended up in the hospital.

"I was just trying to get my purse," Tiffany stuttered. She stood, pointing at the strap that appeared from behind the couch. She slowly moved toward the couch to grab her purse. "What's going on, Brian?" She snatched her purse from behind the couch and took a few steps backward to get out of Brian's reach.

"You were in my bed naked, and now Kayla thinks we had something going on."

Tiffany tried to think of the last thing she could remember from the night before. She remembered taking pictures with Kayla to post on Instagram, then talking and drinking with a few people in the kitchen.

"What?" Tiffany's voice cracked.

"What were you doing naked in my bed?"

"I don't know." Tiffany was scared. She wondered if she was being made fun of. If someone took pictures of her while she was sleep. If someone took advantage of her. Then, she grew angry. "It's your house, Brian. I don't remember any of that. All I know is that I woke up in your bed without any clothes on." Tiffany started to cry. What would people say about her? She was still a virgin, or at least she had hoped. Images were popping up in her head faster than she could think.

"Get out Tiffany." Brian was mad.

Tiffany walked backward toward the door, until she reached the knob. She ran to her car and closed the door. She found her phone in her purse and unlocked it. She had missed four calls and twelve texts from Kayla.

You're probably still with him right now.

I trusted you. I thought we were friends.

Now I know why you didn't want me to sleep with him.

I'll never speak to you again.

Tiffany couldn't read anymore. She called Kayla, but from the short number of rings, she could tell that her call was being ignored.

The time read 12:35. How did she lose so much time?

Tiffany looked through her phone pictures and saw the few snapped photos of her smiling with Kayla. She went to her Instagram page and saw that she was tagged in a collage photo with Kayla. Kayla was kissing her on her cheek. The post read 14 HOURS AGO.

14 hours ago? She had been out for more than half a day.

"Hey, Tiffany. Are you okay?" Her classmate, Ashley, peeled her away from her thoughts.

"Uhm. Yeah. I'm fine." Tiffany took her seat in class next to Ashley.

"Look," Ashley whispered. Tiffany followed Ashley's gaze to the front of the class. Jenna set a stack of books on the teacher's desk and waved at the students. A tall, disheveled man wearing brown glasses waited for her by the door. Tiffany watched as they left the classroom.

"She said her dad is checking her out of school. She's going back to Cincinnati to live with her mom," Ashley said.

"How convenient." Tiffany snarled. Jenna hadn't even been at the school long. Seemed like she came long enough to ruin Tiffany's closest friendships and then leave. Maybe she didn't want to witness the aftermath of the mess that she had made.

Tiffany had met Kayla in middle school. It was right after some girl tried to start a fight with her. Tiffany remembered thinking that Kayla was so cool about the situation. They had been joined at the hip ever since. That was, until Jenna came.

Jenna was just a new student about a month ago, and it seemed she immediately sunk her teeth into Kayla. The first Tiffany had heard of Jenna was during lunch, a few days after she started at Tubman High.

"Hey, everyone. I want you to meet Jenna," Kayla said as they sat at their usual spot in the cafeteria.

Jenna looked unsuspecting at the time. Super skinny, in need of sun, but she wore nice makeup and had long shiny hair. Her clothes seemed a bit expensive, but not out of the ordinary for a high schooler trying to fit in.

"Hi guys." Jenna said. She was seemingly shy, but Tiffany felt different as weeks passed.

After cheer practice one day, Tiffany caught wind of Jenna telling Kayla that she thought Tiffany liked Brian. Jenna kept eyeing Tiffany and Brian as they secretly discussed the logistics of Kayla's surprise designer heels. Tiffany shrugged it off, until she had heard that Jenna accused her of trying to date Brian behind Kayla's back. Since then, she stood clear of Jenna.

"What's Jenna's problem?" Tiffany had asked Kayla in the hallway one day.

"She's just overprotective that's all." Kayla answered.

"Of what? She's known you for like five minutes. If anyone should be overprotective, it would be me," Tiffany responded.

Kayla laughed as if it was nothing. But it was more than nothing. It was a huge accusation, that was funny to Kayla, until Tiffany somehow ended up naked on Brian's bed.

No one had said anything about Tiffany being on Brian's bed. At least there were no pictures, like Tiffany thought. It seemed no one saw but Tiffany, Kayla, Brian, and Jenna. Word got around that Brian may have raped Tiffany. She didn't know how the rumor got started, because she was almost sure that no one saw anything. Tiffany didn't think Brian raped her. Brian assured her that he didn't touch her, but Tiffany didn't know what to believe. She knew that Kayla didn't want to talk to her, Brian didn't want to be near her for fear of accusations, and Jenna scowled at her like she was the scum of the earth. Tiffany would find other friends.

Like Demetrius, she wanted things to go back to normal too, but she had no idea how. She didn't want to talk to Brian or Jenna again. She didn't know how to make things right with Kayla if she did decide to show her face. It was clear that Kayla believed one month of friendship over four years of friendship anyway.

Who would believe that she had been drugged and left naked in Brian's bedroom? It was embarrassing enough. Tiffany was actually relieved that all that came of it was her messing around with Brian. The alternative could have been that she was gang raped by the entire football team, or that she was trying to be a slut. Tiffany hadn't even thought about having sex. It wasn't that she was saving herself for marriage or anything; it was just that she had so many more important things to do than be some guy's girlfriend.

She wanted to win the regional cheer competition. English AP was kicking her butt. The SATs were right around the corner. Choosing a college was time consuming. It was just too much to think about. Sex just wasn't that important. Everyone already thought she was a pretty and mysterious cheerleader anyway. Who was she to tell them different? She'd flirt with guys all the time, but she didn't take any of them seriously. She could hang out with whomever, whenever and not worry about any added pressure. She thought Kayla was on the same page with her until a few weeks before, when she started thinking about having sex with Brian.

"Why is it important right now? Sex will always be there," Tiffany told her.

"I just want it to be special. We've been dating for two years. I think he's waited long enough."

"He's waited? What about you?"

"I'm ready."

"I don't know, Kayla. You don't want to be knocked up and miss out on college like Mitzi did last year."

Kayla laughed, "I'm not Mitzi. I know what a condom is. I'm not stupid."

"Well, I respect your decision. Whatever you want to do. I just don't want you to regret it later."

Kayla smiled at her. She always smiled at her. Kayla treated Tiffany like she was her big sister, asking her for advice. She'd advise her on her next move. Tiffany never understood why Kayla was trying to grow up so fast, but she was going to be supportive no matter what. She just never knew that being supportive would end with her being naked on her best friend's boyfriend's bed. She wanted the whole thing to be behind her.

Tiffany wanted the drama of Harriet Tubman High behind her and wanted to focus on a four-year university, a place where the kids were more than just kids. They were ambitious adults, so focused on their future careers that they had almost missed their future spouses sitting in class right next to them. Where they came from happy backgrounds with 4.0 GPAs and supportive friends. No suspicions of rape, no runaway high school friends, no secret enemies.

Tiffany decided that no matter what, she would focus on her positive future. She'd wish the best for Kayla, even though she ran away from her, and focus on friends who were real friends and shared the same goals that she had.

Again, Ashley interrupted her thoughts. "What do you think about Howard? I got this brochure in the mail over the weekend and it looks pretty cool."

14 ASHLEY

Brian raped Tiffany. By now, everyone knew. Ashley just wasn't sure why Tiffany was so coy about it. She acted like nothing had happened. The only difference between Tiffany before Kayla's party and Tiffany after Kayla's party was that she no longer talked to Brian. And, of course, she no longer talked to Kayla. No one knew where she was. It seemed like she hardly talked to Demetrius anymore, but Ashley had caught them talking before class. Ashley talked to Tiffany often about more important things, such as their future. She decided if Tiffany didn't want to talk about being violated, she wouldn't press it.

Ashley had asked Tiffany about what had happened two weeks before, which was right after she found out about the rape, but Tiffany just shrugged and said nothing. Ashley couldn't help but think if that had happened to her, she would take Brian to court, his parents to court, and even the entire football team if she could.

"See you tomorrow," Ashley called to Tiffany as she raced out of the classroom after the last bell rang.

When she thought back to Kayla's party, she didn't remember anything being out of place. She remembered thinking that Kayla, Jenna, and Tiffany had disappeared at some point, but Ashley was so drunk and high that she could care less. She had just come into the house after passing a blunt around with a few of her classmates when she overheard someone talking to Brian.

"What's going on, Brian?" they had asked.

Brian shook his head. He looked bothered but didn't want to talk. He snatched up one of the liquor bottles from the congregation of bottles on the kitchen table. He lay back on the couch and began to drink.

Wow, who killed his buzz? Ashley thought to herself before taking her position center of the dancefloor. Ashley danced until half of the party was gone. The only reason she left when she did was because her friend, Lil' D, was deejaying and he started packing up. When the DJ left, so did the party.

"That party was so lit!" Ashley said to Jenna the Tuesday following the party.

Jenna was taking books from her locker and putting them into her backpack. "I'm happy you had fun. Seems everyone had fun except the birthday girl." Jenna closed her locker.

"What do you mean? How could she not have fun? It was lit."

"Well." Jenna lowered her voice. "Brian raped Tiffany at the party."

Ashley gasped. "What! Yea, right."

"Kayla doesn't want anyone to know what happened because she's so embarrassed. I mean, when I thought back on it, it had to be a rape because Tiffany was really spacey."

Ashley covered her still opened mouth. "Where's Kayla now? I haven't heard anyone say anything about it."

"That's because no one knows. Kayla told me she had to get away. I'm not sure where she is, but I'm sure she's devastated, but just keep this between me and you. Kayla is so ashamed right now." Jenna left Ashley standing by the lockers in awe.

Ashley had no idea why she told her. Everyone knew she didn't keep secrets.

Ashley didn't want to spread rumors, though, which is why she wanted to first get confirmation from Tiffany. It took almost until the end of the day before Ashley had a chance to speak with Tiffany alone. She saw her walking into the bathroom before the last class period. Ashley walked in after her. She looked under the other stalls to make sure no one else was there with them.

"Hey, Pretty Girl Tiffany," Ashley said to her after she came out of the stall.

"Hey, what's up, Ash."

Ashley stood in front of the mirror, pretending to examine her face.

Tiffany walked up to the sink next to her to wash her hands. "Hey, I heard something really weird and I just wanted to check with you."

"Shoot." Tiffany smiled at her as she turned off the faucet.

"After we were all taking pics and dancing in the middle of the floor, I don't remember seeing you at Kayla's party. Did you leave early?"

Tiffany's smile faded quickly. Ashley could tell that she struck a chord. That was confirmation enough for her.

"Uhm. Yea. I uhm, had to leave." Tiffany dried her hands and turned toward the door. "I have to get to class. See you later, Ashley." Tiffany rushed out of the bathroom. She didn't look back at Ashley or wait for a reply.

Ashley was stunned. She knew he had a temper, but she couldn't believe that Brian was such a monster. Tiffany was too ashamed to even say anything, basically relinquishing her power. Brian could have had any girl he wanted. Why'd he have to rape his girlfriend's best friend? There was no way Brian would keep that cool guy image after Ashley got done with him.

Ashley couldn't do much talking in her last class, but she started texting as soon as she sat down. By Wednesday morning, every person in the school had heard something about Tiffany and Brian. Some said that Brian raped Tiffany and others said that it was consensual, but it was a known fact that something was going on between the two. Yet, both Tiffany and Brian denied it all.

"I know you're a victim, Tiffany, but you have to take back your power," Ashley said to Tiffany the following Monday in class. Ashley had done a lot of research on rape victims. Her sister was a victim of rape and she stood by her side, encouraging her from the minute she had found out. It took almost a year for them to find and prosecute her rapist, and he still got off. Her sister was going to need counseling the rest of her life. "Staying silent gives him power."

"Ashley, I know you're trying to help, but nothing happened between Brian and me. I'm not sure how this rumor got started, but it's simply not true."

Ashley was a little bothered, knowing that she helped to spread the rumor, but she still felt that Tiffany was in denial. She had read about how differently victims would act after their rape. She knew better than to press the issue, and with her not having her best friend to confide in, Ashley decided that being a listening non-judgmental friend was the best that she could offer Tiffany.

Actually, Ashley and Tiffany were more associates than friends. Ashley worked hard over the last two years to not pass judgment on girls like Tiffany and Kayla. They were really smart and beautiful girls, but they were cheerleaders and convinced other girls to be cheerleaders. Ashley thought that women should not allow men to objectify them by being sparkly toy things on the sideline while the men did the heavy lifting. The boys would ogle at the girls in their midriff tops and super short skirts, and the cheerleaders had no problem with it. Often, they would smile and flirt, inviting their objectified image.

Ashley shrugged the thought off. She figured that Tiffany needed a friend during this time, which was more important than any image Tiffany had. No matter what image Tiffany put off, she didn't deserve to be raped. Regardless if Ashley was a friend or an associate, she decided that she'd be there for Tiffany. No one should have to deal with the aftermath of rape alone. Ashley knew that eventually, she'd need someone to confide in.

Kayla had now been missing a full two weeks, and the school was finally getting back to normal. Maybe the vigil worked. At first, Ashley had heard Kayla's name several times in each class period. Her family talked about it at home, and where's Kayla hashtags were all over the 'gram. Since Harriet Tubman tanked at the big game Friday, people kept talking about how Brian's game must have been off because of Kayla's disappearance, but Tubman High still made the playoffs and the whole city was getting into playoff mode. Kayla's disappearance was slowly becoming last week's news.

Ashley quickly walked to the bus stop. Although she hated her job, she couldn't be a minute late. The bus drivers would sometimes arrive and leave her stop early, causing her to wait an additional fifteen minutes. She'd been working at the country club's club house for almost a year and was tired of being nice to overly spoiled business men, lazy housewives, and teens that never had to work a day in their life. Some of them were Tubman students. They reminded her why she had to keep her grades up. She planned to graduate at the top of her class, master college, and start her tech company. That way, she'd never have to answer to another person again.

Ashley looked at her phone and noticed that she had another five minutes before the bus was scheduled to be there. She scrolled through her Instagram feed to kill the time; a bunch of selfies, food pics, and quotes. She was getting tired of seeing the same 'ol things day in and day out. Some people lived for the gram.

$500 for 4 hours of work. Video girl needed.

That post caught Ashley's attention. She clicked on the comments to read the chain. It was posted by Big Weight. He was one of Lil D's clients. Big Weight was a local rapper, but his career was starting to take off. When she started following him last year, he had the same amount of followers that she had. Now, his following had quadrupled.

His comment read: Bitches and Bricks Coming Soon. Need a lead vixen for our shoot this Friday. Our lead went missing. Looking to fill position today. DM for more info. We are screening page images. No response will be given if you're not what we're looking for.

>*Modelkay* Heard your lead was #whereskayla

>*Tashbeens* She probably somewhere high, laughing at ya'll

>*Rasheeda_theone* I'm down. You won't regret it.

The rest of the comments were hopefuls looking for their chance of stardom. $500 to be half dressed as some man's trophy. Ashley closed the app. She couldn't believe how low some women would sell themselves just for men to disrespect them.

Wow. What if Kayla was his lead? Ashley wasn't surprised. It was just like her parading around in a cheerleading skirt. Ashley knew that was the type of attention Kayla liked, not the attention that her boyfriend and Tiffany got.

Suddenly, Ashley did feel bad for Kayla. She wouldn't be the first victim of simply trying to fit in. Ashley really did hope Kayla was off enjoying herself. It was the perfect time. Kayla was seventeen now. No one could make her attend school. She was old enough to get a job. Maybe she started a new life. Ashley was excited thinking about her own countdown to freedom. College would be her new life, and she really believed that it was going to be worth the wait.

15 WAYNE

"These hoes foul." Wayne laughed with his homeboy, Lil' D, about the responses on his Instagram page. "The post says to DM if interested. What's with all these comments?"

"They probably can't read," Lil' D responded. "I thought you had a girl already."

"Man… I had the perfect girl. That chick Kayla that ran a way. I thought she would have come back by now, especially since I had already given her half."

"You gave that chick $250 and she ran off with it?"

"Naw. I gave her $500."

"Wow! She can't be worth the five."

Lil' D knows nothing about business, Wayne thought to himself. Kayla wasn't just a bad bitch; she had a following much larger than they had. She was a marketing move. By the time she posted her pictures on set and promoted the video, they'd have the most views they had ever had.

"We'll never know now," Wayne replied.

"For some reason, that name sounds familiar," Wayne heard Lil' D say.

At first, Wayne took Kayla's disappearance personal. He had secretly stalked her online for months. He couldn't like her pictures because he didn't want to seem thirsty.

He vaguely remembered that Kayla attended the rival high school, Harriet Tubman. It wasn't until he one day saw his buddy, Fontayne checking out her Instagram page that, he paid her any attention.

"Damn! Who is that?" Wayne had asked him.

Fontayne stopped scrolling down his page to ask which picture he was referring to. When Wayne pointed to Kayla's image, he vaguely said, "It's just my neighbor."

"You not trying to holla?"

"I gave up on that senior year."

Wayne found Kayla's page and clicked the follow button. "Damn! Why she got so many followers?" Wayne decided then and there that he needed her in one of his videos.

Fontayne and Wayne went to Moor High School together. Back then, Wayne would freestyle every now and then, but he wasn't the least bit interested in music. When Wayne made it to college without a plan in sight, it was Fontayne who told him to consider majoring in music. Soon after, he learned about a small, local music studio and began to visit it every few weeks. It soon became a ritual; schedule a few writing sessions, hang out at the studio, find other rappers to collab with.

He met his producer, Lil' D, at the local recording studio when he recorded his first hit song, *Do It For Ya Boy*. The song was an instant hit. Lil' D promised that he'd produce more hits, but he'd have to change his name first. He told him no one would take him serious with a name like Wayne. Two blunts later, Lil' D convinced Wayne to take on a new moniker, Big Weight. Wayne thought the name was dumb and only half-jokingly agreed to it. He had no idea that he'd become a regional rap star.

Wayne wasn't stopping at regional, with his new single, Bitches and Bricks, he was going national. Although Lil' D knew absolutely nothing, other than how to make a number one hit, Wayne's business sense, charisma and hustler demeanor were going to take them all the way to the top. He dropped out of college at the end of the last semester so that he could focus on his budding career. Wayne only hoped Lil' D could also stay focused long enough until they got there.

Wayne finished direct messaging two prospects for his video shoot that Friday. "Ay, what time you shutting the shop down today? I got two hoes coming through."

"Soon as White Boy Steve get here, I'm out. 'Less you got a couple for me too."

"Naw, man. They auditioning for the video this Friday."

Lil' D raised one eye brow.

"It's not like that," Wayne assured him. "It's strictly business. I keep telling you, we can play after we get to the top. That's the mistake ya' last rappers made. I'm not following in their footsteps."

Lil' D laughed, "Alright. I'll wait on the talent to see what you working with."

Wayne's phone rang. "What up, dog?" It was Fontayne.

"Aw, nothing man. I saw your IG post. I sure hate Kayla didn't come through for you."

"It's alright, man. You win some, you lose some. So, she still hasn't shown up?"

"Naw, man. Her mom hardly comes out of the house, but when I do see her, she looks sick. I hope she returns soon."

"Be good if she could show up by Friday."

"I know another girl that may be interested, if you want."

"Naw, I got a couple girls coming over in a little. If they don't work out, I'll let you know."

"All right man."

They hung up the phone.

When Wayne finally got the courage to ask Kayla to be in his video, he figured it was best to like the simplest picture she posted, so that she would know it was a professional request. Of course, Wayne wasn't opposed to something more, but he remembered from high school that Kayla was always about business. Her name lived on the Principal's Honor Roll.

Kayla agreed to meet with him the Monday before her birthday. He wanted to be sure to lure her in, so he gave her half up front. He knew she had been modeling for different brands, so she took her IG image very seriously. Basic bitches would get excited about $500, but she was no basic bitch. He needed a yes before she could think of a reason to say no, so he offered her a lot more.

He handed her the money in an envelope. She opened the envelope and counted the money.

"I keep my word."

"I'm not saying you don't, but I'd be a fool not to check," she said with a cute smile.

"Don't stick me for my money now. I expect to see you on time and ready to go."

"I don't have to dance or anything, right? I can choose my own outfit, too?"

"Yes. That's what we agreed to." Wayne had always seen Kayla look flawless. She could do no wrong in his eyes. She was going to be the lead female, so she didn't have to do anything but stand by his side and look pretty.

"Cool. I'll be there. Right on time. Thanks for thinking of me." Kayla reached out her hand to shake Wayne's.

He thought for sure they'd chat for a while, then maybe he could ask her to lunch, but she was cutting their meeting short. He settled on the fact that she'd have to spend hours with him on set during the video. He shook her hand. "Can't wait," he said.

Kayla turned to leave. They'd met around the side of the corner store, so he wasn't sure where she was going and didn't dare look. She was too popular a person for her to think anything about him that wasn't cool. Their only means of communication was Instagram, and he didn't think to direct message her until he heard of her disappearance on the news, that following Tuesday.

Wayne always had a contingency plan. Not that she knew, but he knew where she lived in case she didn't show up. He also knew where her school was and who she hung out with. Never did he think she'd fall off the face of the earth. He messaged her twice more, and still no response. He really hoped she wasn't in danger, but mostly hoped that she showed up, looking flawless on Friday. That would be the surprise of his life. That would surely get major promotion for his video. As far as he was concerned, as long as she was still missing, there was still a chance. A chance until Friday, that was.

"What up, homies!" White Boy Steve walked in loudly as he always had. Wayne hated how he tried to fit in. He heard that he was going around calling himself a low-key boss. He was low-key alright, but nothing was boss about him.

Wayne ignored him and pretended to look for something in a notepad.

"Sup, White Boy Steve!" Lil' D gave him dap.

"The usual, right?"

"I need a lil' extra. Big Weight got some hoes coming by later. We want to make sure they have a good time."

Wayne looked up. "Naw. Me and my hoes don't need that shit. Don't put us in that, D."

White Boy Steve and Lil' D looked at Wayne as if they were offended. "He a square. Just give me the usual," Lil' D barked.

"That party was lit, wasn't it," White Boy Steve said to Lil' D.

"Ay, man. Thanks again for hooking me up with that gig." Lil' D laughed, "I was so high, though, man. I barely even remember that night."

"Yea, I noticed."

Wayne ignored the conversation and transaction between Lil' D and White Boy Steve. Wayne wasn't one to judge, but he hated Lil' D's drug habits. Usually, they didn't affect business, so he tried not to get involved. It was like Lil' D had to try every new drug on the market. He wasn't too fond of White Boy Steve either. He didn't like how popular he became after his boy Jackson went to jail. Wayne didn't trust him, so he wouldn't even talk when he was around. He decided that he'd just write until it was time to choose the star of his video.

16 FONTAYNE

Fontayne was leaving for work on Tuesday morning when he caught a glimpse of Ms. Washington. She looked like death. Her eyes were sunken into her head, dark spots began to appear in several areas on her face, and her hair was matted. Fontayne wasn't a huge fan of Kayla, but he really wished she would return for the sake of her mom. He was sure that Ms. Washington wore the same oversized house dress that she wore when he saw her last week. His only sight of Ms. Washington was when she fetched the mail.

She is probably hoping there was a sign from Kayla in that mailbox, Fontayne thought to himself. Word on the street was that Kayla had run away, but apparently, her mom didn't seem to believe that. Either that, or she just missed her daughter.

Fontayne remembered the last time he had seen Kayla. He was smoking in the back yard and saw her sneaking out of the back door the night before she disappeared. She had done that three times that week alone. Now that he thought about it, Kayla was probably practicing for her run away. He didn't know where she was going or why, but it seemed to be new behavior for her.

He didn't talk to Kayla often after he graduated high school. She used to smile and wave at him a few years before, when he was the lead scorer on the Moorish Knights basketball team. They had a cute rivalry like the rest of the school, but it was laced with flirting. He knew Kayla had been dating a football player from her school, but that didn't matter to him. He was a senior at the time and in his eyes, he could date any girl he wanted. He was even dating the white girl across town at the country's most prestigious private school.

Fontayne had just accepted a full ride scholarship to play basketball on a NCAA championship team out of state. He would joke with Kayla about how she could come visit him and she'd always smile when he said it. He didn't make it through the summer before she started looking at him different. Everyone started looking at him different.

He was enjoying his last couple weeks at home before leaving for school when he caught a case. His boy, Jackson, supplied the whole neighborhood. Fontayne knew that it wasn't a good idea to hang with him because he didn't want anything to do with drugs, but they had been friends since elementary. Jackson was his biggest fan. Jackson dropped out of school before their sophomore year and worked his way up the drug dealing ladder. He was a busy guy, but he always made time to attend Fontayne's basketball games. He told Fontayne to keep his hands clean because he knew that he was looking forward to his college graduation. He joked about how he had never dated a college chick before, but he'd be on campus all the time once Fontayne went to college.

One summer weekend, after Fontayne's high school graduation, Jackson took Fontayne to visit his girlfriend on the other side of town. At the time, Jackson was Fontayne's only access to a car. Jackson never liked driving to the other side of town, and even though he didn't like the idea of Fontayne dating that girl, he knew how much he liked visiting her. Her parents were always gone and she didn't have any limits. Jackson was always careful when driving into uncommon territory. He drove a clean, registered car, took no extra weapons, and kept no drugs on him. He didn't need a reason for them to get into any trouble.

Fontayne and Jackson hadn't been in his girlfriend's house twenty minutes before her dad barged in with the police close behind. Before the boys could even speak, the officers had them face down on the living room floor.

"Daddy! What are you letting them do to my friends?"

"These thugs are no friends of yours," her dad berated. "Get these criminals out of my house."

The officers dragged Jackson and Fontayne to the front lawn, where the neighbors stood watch. To make matters worse, Fontayne forgot that he left two joints in the passenger door of the car. It was just the ammunition the police needed to further harass the boys. The officers destroyed Jackson's car searching for more. That, coupled with Jackson's record, the officers figured they had probable cause to remove seats and the door linings to gather evidence. Jackson's car was destroyed.

Four months and $50,000 later, they were able to beat the case, but Fontayne had to kiss college goodbye. It was like Fontayne let the whole town down. To Garvey, he was going to be their local hero. He was going to swing by college before making it pro and end up with the keys to the city. They'd name buildings after him, he'd start programs for youth, and shine a global spotlight of their entire city. He wrecked it for the whole town. He couldn't go anywhere without hearing people whisper.

That's what he gets, messing with them white girls.

I knew sooner or later, him being friends with that dealer would catch up to him.

He thought he was above everything. Even the law.

The girl's daddy said that Fontayne tried to rape that girl, and I wouldn't put it past him.

That boy is gon' be a burden to his mama for the rest of her days.

Fontayne had to make a name for himself. Even though he wasn't found guilty of anything, he felt branded for life. If he didn't feel like he owed it to his mom, he would have left town immediately. Not only did he owe it to his mom, but he also owed Jackson.

Even when he was owed an *I told you so* from him, never once did Jackson seem upset with Fontayne. He didn't ask for one penny back from lawyer fees or his destroyed car. Jackson only apologized to him that he would never get to play ball on national TV.

It took over a year, but Fontayne got his welding certification and was finally making a decent income. He paid off his mom's home, bought her a new car, and even paid her medical bills, but the people in town still looked down on him. Including Kayla. He was used to it now, so it didn't bother him as much.

Fontayne spent a lot of time in his backyard smoking. His favorite spot was in a chair, underneath the tree's shadow. It was relaxing there because seated away from the dim porchlight, no one would bother him because they didn't realize that he was there. The added plus was that he could see his neighbors through their chain linked fences and occasionally hear their conversations. He wasn't looking for gossip, but it was still amusing nonetheless.

He watched a few weeks ago, when some skinny little white girl met up with Kayla in her backyard. She was crying about a beating that her father had given her. Kayla ran to the rescue with this huge case of makeup to help her cover it up. He wanted to tell Kayla not to trust her because she reminded him a lot of his ex-girlfriend who pretended to care but wouldn't speak a word to defend him in court. Fontayne had to sit and listen to that girl lie to Kayla for almost half an hour. If he so much as moved an inch, they would have known that he was listening.

He had learned a lot about reading people from Jackson. It was like Jackson had a PhD in everything that wasn't academics, and he loved to teach those skills to others. The only person Fontayne figured he couldn't read was White Boy Steve.

Fontayne saw how he taught White Boy Steve the ins and outs of his business. Although Fontayne couldn't prove it, he was sure that White Boy Steve set him up. He questioned White Boy Steve about it once, and he gave that same shifty look and fast talk that he saw the skinny white girl giving Kayla. Fontayne felt sure that he read both the girl and White Boy Steve correctly, but his boy Wayne would often joke that he was simply suffering from PTSD after what he went through with his girlfriend; that maybe he was just extra suspicious of people since then.

Fontayne saw Kayla meet that girl twice more, right before he saw her for the last time. The last time though, the white girl wasn't there, and she'd caught him looking because the sun hadn't quite set yet.

Fontayne was putting out his cigarette when Kayla jumped out a red Dodge at the end of the alley the Sunday night before she went missing. The car looked exactly like the car her boyfriend owned, except it wasn't. He'd caught a glimpse of the license plate number, and it was completely different. Also, the driver was much shorter than her boyfriend, but then again, everyone was much shorter than her boyfriend.

"What?" Kayla snarled with an attitude on her quick strut past his backyard to hers.

"Was just wondering how come he didn't just drop you off at the front."

"Stay out of my business. Brian has things to do."

Fontayne didn't respond. He just eyed her as she slipped into the backdoor of her home. Clearly, she thought he was an idiot. The guy in the car wore a Cincinnati Bengals hat. No one, anywhere in Garvey was a fan, especially her football playing boyfriend. She must have been cheating on her boyfriend and since she was slipping out the back, she must've also lied to her parents. She'd always met her boyfriend in the front.

Fontayne had left that next morning to visit Jackson out of state. Although the travel was costly and time consuming, he did it every month to show his continued support. He returned home just in time to learn that she was missing from the new Garvey Morning News Thursday morning.

"Mom? Is this the Kayla that lives next door?"

"I'm afraid so. Her folks have been questioning the whole neighborhood since Monday. They'll probably be knocking on the door again this morning."

His mom continued to mumble about him apparently missing a search party and something about the neighbors getting involved. He stopped listening to her and pulled up Kayla's Instagram page. He knew how active she was on the app. He clicked on her last picture to see a long list of where's Kayla hashtags. One post said if you have any information, contact Detective Madison. His telephone number was posted.

Fontayne knew it was a long shot, but he decided to call to give information about the car he saw her leave. It's not like she went missing Sunday night. She did return home, and she was doing so by her own free will, but it was all he had.

"Hello," a lady answered sounding annoyed.

"I'm calling for Detective Madison."

"He's busy, but I can take your message."

He told the lady about the car, the license plate number that he remembered, and about that ugly Cincinnati Bengals hat. She sounded disinterested, but she took his information and promised that she'd get it to Detective Madison.

Fontayne didn't know if he felt like a snitch or good that he was helping out. He knew Kayla would be pissed if he told someone about her cheating on her boyfriend. At least this way, the police could look into it and if they reached her and she resurfaced, her mom would come back from the dead and wouldn't know that he had anything to do with it.

17 WHITE BOY STEVE

White Boy Steve loved being the token white kid at Tubman High school, and now, since his mentor was out of the picture, he wasn't just the token kid; he had grown to be the token dealer at all the schools in the district. Jackson had first hired Steve so that he could settle his debt, but Steve's interest and capital soon took off. It seemed no one of authority suspected him as a dealer. He was blowing up, so much so that he was considering getting his own workers.

"Steven," his father called. "I need these papers completed by Thursday. We're visiting the school on Friday."

"Yes, sir."

White Boy Steve had no interest in college, but his father had already made plans for him to work at his firm, and there was no telling his father no. Steve loved the independence that making his own money gave him. He loved the respect that he received from the people around town. He didn't want to mess that up. He didn't want to answer to his father or men like his father, but he was just too afraid to tell his father no.

Steve took the $5,000 that he made the night before from his backpack and put it into his safe in the back of his closet. He left to grab the college papers that his dad wanted him to fill out.

Steve thumbed through the stack of papers on his father's desk. "All of this?" Steve questioned in disbelief.

"It's an application for college, not an application for McDonald's. You can complete it, can't you?"

His dad was perpetually condescending. Steve didn't think his dad knew how not to be. Every time he spoke to him, he belittled him. He didn't even know why his dad wanted him to work for him.

"You need an essay too. You might want to get started on that now." His dad began typing on his computer. Steve knew that was his cue to leave.

Steve wasn't worried one bit about getting his essay done, or the application completed. He'd just pay Jo to do it for him. He found out how smart Jo was his freshman year and had been paying her to do his work ever since.

Steve felt as if his dad always thought he was a disappointment. He attended the most prestigious private school in the country, which happened to be two blocks away from his house, but he just couldn't make the grades. For fear that his grades would affect college, his dad enrolled him into Tubman High, thinking that he'd easily outrank the students in the public school, but his dad didn't do his research. The classes were just as difficult, if not more rigorous than the private school, and he was struggling there as well.

When he brought his first report card home, his dad beat him so bad that he had broken his arm. Since then, he used his allowance to influence his classmate ,Jo, to help him keep his grades up. His dad never questioned him again. Steve texted Jo:

Jo, I need an essay by this evening

> *No problem, send me the requirements*

Steve scanned and emailed the entire application to Jo. She never had a problem doing his work or having his deadlines because he paid her so well. The moment he received the work back, he'd make a deposit into her bank account. Technology made everything so easy. He knew she'd have it back to him by the time school was over.

Steve refilled his backpack with product, added in his college application, and headed to his car for his long commute to school.

"Steve, I need to get something from you before you go." His neighbor flagged him down before he exited the gated community. Steve already knew what he wanted. It wasn't the first time Brock flagged him down on his way to school.

He removed a small inconspicuous package from his glovebox. "Here you go, Brock."

"I'll take care of you on your way back home." Brock always told

Steve that, but he never paid him. Steve didn't mind, though, because Brock was the reason his income tripled. He helped to get Jackson sent away.

Steve worked for Jackson for months. He mimicked his every action, met each of his connects, and almost became his right-hand man. Steve found out when and where Jackson's next big order was and tipped off Brock, who was then a rookie police officer. Steve pretended to be surprised when it all happened and made sure to donate money to his legal fees to make it all seem legit, but in reality, Steve was expanding his own personal empire, and it seemed no one suspected him.

"Don't worry about it, Brock."

"Hey. I saw on the news this weekend about that girl that ran away. She was nice." Brock gave the thumbs up to show his approval. "I see why you like that school. I might need to come by sometimes."

Steve smiled, then drove away. He laughed at Brock's comment. He knew that there was no way that anyone from his neighborhood would step foot near Harriet Tubman.

It took a while, but Steve became comfortable with his daily commute. He used it as a time to think. None of the other students seemed to notice that he didn't live in their area. His dad owned a property in Garvey that he'd let to anyone for upfront cash. He used that property as his address, and he frequented every major hangout. Other than that, everyone just thought he was conspicuous simply because he was a dealer. He was convinced that his cover couldn't be blown. Even if it was, his dad had ties with the police chief, the DA and the mayor. Steve felt untouchable.

Steve completed a few transactions on his way to his locker, as he did every morning he came to school.

"Hey, White Boy Steve!" Jo called to him in the hallway near his locker.

"What's up, Jo? Sorry about the last-minute assignment."

"No, it's cool. I should actually be finished by lunch."

"Hey, have you seen Jenna around?" Steve asked. He just remembered his new favorite customer. She'd see him every other day, but he hadn't seen her since the football game before the vigil.

"Who?" Jo asked.

"New student. Skinny white girl. She used to hang with Kayla."

Jo thought for a minute. "Oh. I remember someone saying that the new student left. That must be her."

"Man... I'm going to miss her."

Jo eyed Steve curiously.

Steve laughed, "It's not like that. She was becoming my biggest customer. She was even bringing me new customers."

Jo put her fingers in her ears while humming a tune and walked off.

Steve laughed to himself. He forgot that Jo told him she never wanted to hear any details of his *business*. The less she knew, the less she could say.

Jenna found Steve the first day she attended the school. Word traveled fast to the students where they could get their poison of choice.

"Hey!" She walked up to him with her head down and her face hidden underneath a pink hoodie.

"What you need?" White Boy Steve knew not to use too many words when talking to customers.

"I don't know. A joint maybe."

He slid her a small manila envelope and she slid him some cash.

"I'm here all week." He said that to encourage his customers to seek him often and did Jenna seek him often. She started buying weed, then pills, then coke. Lastly, she started asking for Ketamine. He could tell she wasn't from around there because she wanted things that no one else had asked for, so much so that Steve thought about including it in his available variety.

Steve suddenly remembered the last time he had seen Kayla was with Jenna. Sunday night after Kayla's birthday party, he met Jenna near the corner store.

"You want the usual?" he asked Jenna. He prided himself on remembering his customer's variety of choice. He thought it made them feel special; that and the fact that he'd reward their loyalty with something extra to try.

"Sure. I'm trying to lift my girl's spirits."

Steve followed Jenna's glance toward Kayla. Kayla was laughing and talking to a short guy wearing a hideous Bengals cap. Steve had never seen him before. He figured that he must have been one of Jenna's friends. "Oh yea? She's trying these too?"

Jenna smiled. "Me and my girl trying to get lit."

"Well, y'all have fun then," Steve said as he stuffed his money in his pocket. Steve turned to walk away, until he heard a pair of high heels.

Kayla walked up to Jenna, whispering loudly. "What's this about a party? I gotta get home."

"What?" Jenna looked confused. "Let me see what he's talking about." Jenna left to talk to the guy.

Steve noticed the expensive pair of shoes that Kayla wore. "Oh wow. Is that shoe porn?" Steve asked her. Everyone who followed Kayla's page knew about her expensive shoe fetish.

Kayla looked down at the shoes with a sheepish smile.

"You wanna pose for the 'gram?" Steve asked.

Kayla shrugged. "Sure".

He took her picture next to the wall of the corner store. He made sure to get her shoes in the picture. She flashed a pretty smile and posed with a peace sign. She did that like she was already famous.

"I'll make sure to put hashtag shoe porn Sunday. Those are dope."

"Ooh. Great idea. I should use that hashtag too."

"Alright, see you later."

Steve hardly talked to Kayla. She didn't usually hang around his type, but he was hoping her new friend would change that. He had forgotten about the picture he took until he one day saw the where's Kayla hashtag. He posted the picture, not knowing how much trouble it could get him in.

As soon as he made it to school the next day, detectives were there waiting on him. His heart was racing at the sight of them, but he knew better than to look guilty.

"These detectives would like to talk to you for a minute," Principal McNair said when he walked into his office.

Steve thought about the drugs in his backpack. He thought about the money in his locker. He thought about all of the people he served that morning and the evening before. He didn't know what could have triggered it.

"We'd like to ask you about Kayla Carlisle," one of the detectives said.

Steve was relieved. He really hoped it didn't show on his face. He sat in one of the empty chairs while the detectives stood watching him, one staring at him intently, while the other was looking at his phone.

Principal McNair sat in his seat behind his desk, concerned. Steve knew not to worry because he had heard that several students had already talked to the detectives and the principal about Kayla.

"I hardly ever talked to her but ask whatever you'd like."

They asked about that picture. Kayla posted pictures all day, every week and they asked him about his one picture. He knew it was a reason he hardly participated on social media. He thought he was doing a nice thing, paying homage to a beautiful girl that had gone missing, but instead, he was making himself out to be a suspect. The last place he needed to be was anybody's suspect.

He didn't know much about Kayla, but everyone really liked her, so he guessed it was a horrible thing that she had gone missing, but while everyone was missing Kayla, he was really going to miss her friend. He ordered all that Ketamine for nothing.

18 JO

Jo made it to Mrs. Jacobs' class right before the bell rang. She began copying the lesson that was written on the board but was interrupted by her buzzing phone. Jo was reluctant to answer the phone because Mrs. Jacobs would confiscate the student's phones if she saw them looking at it. Her phone buzzed a second time, then a third time. Everyone she knew, knew that she was in class. Jo waited until Mrs. Jacobs began talking to a student.

She glanced at her phone and saw that she had four messages from her cousin, Jess. She clicked to open the message after ensuring that Mrs. Jacobs was still preoccupied. The first was a screenshot of an Instagram page. Before Jo could click on the image, three more messages came through. *"What could be so important,"* Jo thought.

Someone's phone rang in the back of the class and, as if on cue, Mrs. Jacobs could be heard saying, "Give it to me now."

Jo glanced to see Mrs. Jacobs speed to the back of the class.

She tapped to open the image. It was Kayla's Instagram page. There was a selfie of her in shades and a purple shirt.

Jo heard more phones buzzing, and students began to whisper around her.

Jo read the caption of the photo. *Sorry to cause so much worry. I just needed a break. After all, I am an ADULT now. I'm going incognito for a while. See you soon.* 💋💋💋

"I told y'all that girl ran away," Jo heard someone say.

Suddenly, the class grew loud with everyone giving their opinions of Kayla and her Instagram post. News traveled fast.

Jo looked at her cousin's messages that were coming in a mile a minute.

> *I don't believe it.*
>
> *That's not her.*
>
> *Why does she have on shades?*
>
> *That's not even how she does her makeup.*
>
> *Someone needs to tell her parents. Or that Detective Madison that her mom talked about.*
>
> *I should call shouldn't I.*

Jo couldn't believe what her cousin was saying. She always joked that Jess was obsessive over Kayla, but she couldn't believe what she was saying. She wrote her back:

Really. Now, you do a better job than the police? You really are obsessed.

"Wow. She already has like 2,000 likes," someone said.

Everyone is obsessed with Kayla, Jo thought. Jo's phone buzzed again. She looked at Jess's message.

> *I'm not obsessed. I just noticed is all.*

Jo knew that Jess hated being called obsessed, so she sent a softer a response.

It's not just you. Everyone in class is going crazy. They said she has like 2,000 likes.

Jo looked around the class. Everyone was looking at their phone. Even Mrs. Jacobs returned to her desk and was now focused on her phone. Jo felt she had no choice but to look at Kayla's page too.

She opened Instagram on her phone. Jo had to admit it, it was odd that Kayla had on shades. She loved showing off her makeup. Jo looked at the growing comments.

Jasoncarter Nice Raybans

That explained it, Jo thought, Kayla was a label whore. The likes on Kayla's post were now at 6,000. Apparently, her disappearance made her even more popular, which Jo used to think was impossible. Jo put her phone away. She realized that she was going to be the only one doing work in class. She finished Steve's essay and college application before the class bell rang again.

When lunch came, Jo met with Steve at his locker. "Here ya go, buddy." She slapped his papers in his hand then continued to the lunch room. Before she reached the lunch line, her phone buzzed. Her bank notified her of the $400 deposited in her account. Jo smiled. *A bonus*, she thought.

"What's up, chica?" Tasha said as she joined her in line.

"Sup." Thinking of Tasha's current hate of Kayla, Jo spoke before Tasha could respond. "I don't want to hear anything else about Kayla. That's all people have been talking about all morning."

"There's nothing else to say, really. She's already deactivated her page. Guess she's gone for good now." Tasha couldn't conceal her smile.

Jo shook her head. Tasha was such a hater.

"Hey, cutie."

Jo turned around to see who was talking, and to whom. Brian was standing behind Tasha, smiling at her. Tasha turned her back to him, trying not to smile. Jo remembered how much Tasha would talk about Brian when they were freshmen. She always figured that's why Tasha didn't like Kayla. Apparently, Kayla got to Brian before she could.

"I like your haircut," Brian said.

Tasha was still facing Jo in line. Jo decided not to be a part of their cat and mouse game. She grabbed her food and found her seat while leaving Tasha and Brian behind to flirt with each other. Jo was happy that at least things could go back to normal. Maybe better than normal. Tasha was gleaming. Steve had given her a bonus, everybody wouldn't be so sad now that they would receive closure from Kayla. It was a going to be a good week.

Tasha finally joined Jo at the table.

"I guess everyone is over Kayla's disappearance." Jo glanced at Brian while Tasha took her seat across from her.

"I thought we weren't talking about Kayla." Tasha smirked.

"What's he talking about?"

"He wants to take me out, of course," Tasha grinned.

"And, what did you say?"

All of Tasha's teeth appeared. She began to eat her lunch.

"You said yes, didn't you?"

"I just told him to call me."

Jo shook her head.

"What?"

"I just know how much you like him. I'm happy for you."

Tasha didn't respond. She started eating her lunch. Jo didn't know how happy she was for Tasha. It felt really weird that Brian would ask her out the same day his missing girlfriend reappeared, but she didn't want to be the hater. She decided that she'd try to be happy for her. She wanted to talk about Brian's anger issues and maybe throw in Kayla's sudden Instagram post, but she didn't want to wipe the smile off her best friend's face.

Ashley sat at the table next to Jo. "Hey, girls," she said.

"Hey," both Jo and Tasha offered.

"Did y'all hear about Kayla?"

Jo rolled her head toward Ashley. She looked at her annoyingly.

"She deactivated her page."

Jo sighed. "Didn't she say she was going to deactivate it?"

"Her caption said, *Incognito.* So, I guess you're right."

"Well, I'm just happy everyone will stop being so worried," Tasha said. "They can just move on with their lives."

Jo cut her eyes at Tasha. She knew that she was referring to Brian.

"It just seems so out of character, though." Ashley added.

"I think it seems in character," Tasha mumbled on top of her chewing.

Jo dropped her fork. She looked from Ashley to Tasha. "Can we just eat?"

Ashley shrugged. Tasha took in another bite. Jo already knew that she had to listen to the conspiracy theories from her cousin when she got home. She wanted to be spared the rest of the day.

She wondered if she'd have to hear that much gossip when she finally made to college. If the whole school would be caught up in the other student's whereabouts. If they'd come up with theories about people's best friends and boyfriends and parents.

Jo was annoyed with hearing only the sound of Tasha and Ashley smacking. She sighed again. She supposed that the talk of Kayla's deactivation wouldn't be the talk of the town anymore soon, so what was the harm in indulging just for today?

"I just wonder how she's going to keep her grades up missing school so long," Jo said.

19 DETECTIVE JOHNSON

"Case closed." Detective Johnson closed the Kayla Carlisle file that sat on his desk.

"And it's about time too," Detective Madison added. "Think I'll finally get home early enough to enjoy my household. I'll see you tomorrow."

"See ya' partner."

Detective Johnson was always happy to close a case file, so he was happy too, but not as happy as Detective Madison. Detective Madison had been a detective for more than twenty years. He had the gut instinct that Detective Johnson hoped to attain. Although both detectives wanted to complete good, quality work, they were different. Detective Madison just wanted to work until he reached retirement, while Detective Johnson was vying to make chief.

That's why he was extra careful on any case that he worked. There was no way to make chief, by making mistakes. He intended to do his due diligence on every case no matter how small it seemed. As soon as the detectives received the case, Detective Madison was skeptical.

"Here ya' go fellas. It's all yours." Their boss dropped the Kayla Carlisle file onto Detective Madison's desk and kept walking. Detective Madison opened the file to see one simple sheet of paper. It was the case details, which didn't have many details.

"Missing teen?" Detective Madison turned the sheet over to make sure nothing was on the back of it. "Why, chief?" Detective Madison dropped the sheet on Detective Johnson's desk, who immediately began hacking at his computer.

"Says here she went missing from school." Detective Johnson collected all the information they needed to talk with Kayla's closest family and friends.

Although Detective Madison wasn't too thrilled about the case, they were covering good ground. By the time the Garvey News broke the story, they had talked to both of Kayla's parents, her neighbors and most of her friends. They had just gotten her last friend, Janice Tayler to agree to come down, the evening the story broke. That was when things got too busy.

"I've never seen this much fuss over a missing teen," Detective Madison told him. "After this interview today I thought we'd be done. What's with all these calls?"

Looking up from his computer, Detective Johnson responded, "That's the power of social media."

"What do you mean?"

"This little girl is well known all over the city. Everyone is concerned. We have more than her family to answer to now."

"Don't they understand there's no suspicion of foul play?"

"Oh shit. I see what happened." Detective Johnson was perusing Kayla's Instagram page. It had became a habit since they got the case. It's where he found most of his leads. "Her mom posted your number in the comments."

"How many people can see that." Detective Madison rushed to look over Detective Johnson's shoulder at his computer.

"Apparently thousands have been on this page."

"Shit!" Detective Madison returned to his desk.

Detective Johnson's desk phone rang. "Yea," he answered.

"Janice Tayler is here," the secretary said on the other end.

Detective Johnson hung up the phone. "Let's go partner," he said to Detective Madison.

The detectives didn't think they'd find much from Kayla's friend, Jenna. They had already heard from Kayla's other friends that they didn't know where she was and that was basically the same response they got from Jenna as well.

Daily, Detective Johnson checked Kayla's social media pages, her debit card and her cell phone. It was like she fell off the face of the earth. There were no surveillance cameras at Tubman High and the disagreements between her friends were insignificant. All of her friends had an alibi. Even the drug dealing white boy at the school, who posted a picture of her on Sunday night, was sitting right in class when she allegedly went missing.

There was only one-time Detective Johnson thought they may have had something.

"Some guy named Big Weight. I don't know him. He's not one of Kayla's friends, but they talked about meeting up."

"I'll look into it Ms. Washington, please try to get some rest."

Ms. Washington didn't know it, but Detective Johnson was already exploring that avenue. They learned that Big Weight was actually a Mr. Wayne Jones. When Ms. Washington called, Detective Johnson was awaiting surveillance footage from the owner of the recording studio Mr. Jones frequented with his junkie friend, Lil D'. Both gentlemen were at the studio during the time that Kayla Carlisle came up missing.

Detective Johnson felt they had left no stone unturned. It really bothered him seeing Ms. Washington crying when they told her that there was nothing else they could do with the case, but he felt she needed to start seeking some type of closure. He assured her that they'd continue to work the file, but they had already questioned everyone who was remotely involved with Kayla.

Detective Johnson had even convinced Detective Madison to join him at the big football game that would include a vigil in Kayla's honor. They made it to the game early, and found perfect seats on the Tubman High school side.

"I can't believe I let you drag me here. My kids will be pissed if they find out I came and didn't bring them," Detective Madison complained.

"We'll just hang out until after the vigil is all."

The cheerleaders came out hooting and hollering at the crowd as soon as the players took the field. They spotted them instantly. Demetrius and Tiffany were the least spirited among all of them. They went with the motions of cheering, but they looked as happy as dying dogs.

"Looks like someone lost their best friend," Detective Madison whispered.

Detective Johnson looked around the crowd, searching for familiar faces or anything out of the ordinary. He spotted a girl at the end of the bleachers. Detective Johnson could only see a corner of her smile and the left side of her eye. She had her arm up with her phone trying to capture the moment with friends. It was a pose he had seen all too much. She was taking a selfie. He stared at the girl, while nudging Detective Madison's arm.

"You think that's her?" Detective Madison whispered to him.

"Let's see."

"Ohhhhh," the crowd sang in unison. Brian had just thrown his third interception. All of the fans were pissed. Detective Madison followed Detective Johnson down the bleachers toward the selfie takers. As soon as they got within ten feet of the girl, she finally stopped taking pictures. Detective Johnson gave her a quick smile when she made eye contact with him, then turned down the aisle to exit the bleacher stands.

"What's wrong?" Detective Madison asked when they reached the bottom of the bleachers.

"It's not her. That's that stalker chic. Just Jess. Remember?"

"Damn," Detective Madison laughed, "How'd you remember her face?"

Detective Johnson thought JustJess was a crazy stalker and had looked her up too. It turned out she was just a super fan of another teenage girl. She was also in class during the disappearance, but she didn't have the means or the motive. As weird as she was, she also had pull with the youngsters. She was the one who started the where's Kayla hashtag. He didn't want to alert her of their presence.

While beneath the bleachers, Detective Johnson decided to grab some snacks from the concession stand. That's where he saw Jenna arguing with a guy.

"You're so dumb Jay, I'm telling you – " she stopped in mid-sentence. "Oh. Hi, Detectives."

The gentleman she was with looked from Detective Johnson to

Detective Madison, then lowered his head. He had tanned skin, dark brown eyes, and looked to be about 5' 6 and 145 pounds.

"Is everything alright here?" Detective Johnson asked.

"Uhm. Yes. My boyfriend didn't get me the cheese fries."

Detective Madison left Detective Johnson's side to get in line at the concession stand. Detective Johnson looked up at Jenna's boyfriend. "You can't forget those cheese fries, man." The guy looked up at him with a smirk. He looked like a scolded puppy. "The Bengals? Really?" Detective Johnson asked.

"Uhm. Yea. It's not mine. I borrowed it from a friend," he replied in a grating voice.

"You might want to give that back." Detective Johnson joined Detective Madison in the concession line, making a mental note to remember to get himself some cheese fries.

The detectives passed by Steve's horrible attempt to hide a drug deal on their way back to their seats in the bleachers in time to watch the half-time show. That is when Principal McNair took the stage to start the vigil for Kayla. Everyone in the stands collected their candles. Nothing seemed out of ordinary. Aside from the vigil, it was just like any other high school game. The detectives left immediately after.

Ms. Washington and Mr. Carlisle had painted a picture of Kayla being a perfectly happy girl who had no reason to run away. Unfortunately, the detectives discovered that that was a lie. Kayla's friends had betrayed her, her dad had betrayed her, and some suspected her of using drugs. After seeing the picture that the school drug dealer posted of her, the detectives had every reason to believe that it was true. Detective Johnson had a psychologist explain to Ms. Washington that traumatic incidents could have altered Kayla's normal behavior. A girl who had built a perfect online image. He simply thought she left before the walls surrounding that image came tumbling down.

Kayla's purse, computer, and phone were all gone. Important things to a teenage girl. Nothing was out of place in her room and her father said that she had so many clothes, it was impossible to know if she had taken some of them or not.

High school drama was what both Detective Madison and Detective Johnson hated the most. The rumors and, mess would now be behind them. They could focus their efforts on real cases. Truly they were done with Kayla before she posted her last Instagram picture. Detective Johnson could picture her resurfacing as one of those traveling girls. Maybe she'd start a new page, titled *Kayla's Adventures*. Who knew? What Detective Johnson was sure of, though, was that the teenage drama was behind him - at least, until the next teenage case.

20 JENNA

"There, it's done." Jenna handed her dad Kayla's phone after posting her last message on Instagram.

"You put us in a lot of shit, Jenna," he said angrily as he dropped the phone on the concrete. He repeatedly stomped the phone until it was unrecognizable. "That was too close for comfort."

Jenna hated his southern drawl. He sounded like a cowboy whose mouth was full of snuff. She walked toward the car before his anger got the best of him. She was looking to put him in a better mood before they made it back to the highway. "You heard Jay. She's made more money in the last two weeks than most girls make in months. She was worth the risk."

Her dad cut his eyes at her only for a second. She could tell that he was calculating the gain. When he slid back into the driver's seat and put the car in gear, she could tell that he agreed. Had he not agreed, she would have collected a few blows to the head before the car ever moved.

161

Jenna tried not to look too happy sitting in the passenger seat, but she was really proud of herself. With all the people she'd help her dad collect, she was steadily increasing their income, which meant she was gaining more power over her dad. She figured she could be running his operation soon. She had come a long way since he found her fourteen years ago.

Jenna was sitting at a park bench near her elementary school, like she did most evenings. She dreaded going home every day because she'd often find her mom passed out from whatever drugs she had taken. That, or she'd have some guy waiting for her to do him a favor. Hardly was home something she looked forward to, so she was in no rush to get back there. Her dad sat down next to her on the park bench.

"Hi, little lady."

"Hi."

"What are you doing out here all by yourself? Shouldn't you be playing with your friends."

"I don't have any." Jenna never looked at the man. She just stared in the distance while answering his questions.

"Surely you have to have some friends. Well, shouldn't you be getting home soon? It's almost supper time."

"We don't have any food, so there's no rush."

"But, aren't you hungry?"

"Got no money."

"Here you go, honey." Her dad reached into his pocket and gave her four twenty-dollar bills. It was the most money Jenna had ever seen at one time.

Jenna was shocked, but didn't want to seem overly excited. Her mom would let men come over all the time to do uncomfortable things to her. They'd always leave a few dollars. She didn't want to think about what she'd have to do for four twenty-dollar bills.

"Here ya' go, honey. Get you something to eat. Buy groceries if you want."

Jenna looked at the money, then she finally looked up at the man. He was skinny, with thin lips and thin hair. He reminded her of herself. She imagined he was how her real dad looked.

"What I gotta do for that?"

"Just smile," he said. "A pretty little girl like you shouldn't walk around hungry. You should be happy. Just smile."

No one had ever called Jenna pretty before. Not unless they wanted her to do something for them. She figured they were in a big park with a lot of people around; what was the harm? She gave him the biggest smile she could think of. He smiled back at her and shoved the money into her hands. She took it, then the man walked away.

At first, she thought she should run after him. Maybe ask him more questions. She sat on the bench for another twenty minutes to make sure nothing else was going to happen, just in case the man was coming back to collect. He didn't. Jenna ran as fast as she could to the nearest fast food restaurant and purchased a feast. She ordered everything she could ever dream of and set it all at the table. She knew that she must have looked like a zoo animal, but she didn't care. She thought she'd never get a day like that again.

After the school the next day, she went back to the same park and sat on the same bench. After hours had passed, she thought the man wasn't going to return, but he had finally shown up. She talked to him for a while and made him promise to meet her at that same park every day. It was the first time she had met a man who didn't want anything from her. He'd just make sure she ate, have a conversation with her, and leave. She told him about her life at school and at home. He'd always tell her that she was pretty and smart. She felt inspired just seeing him.

By the end of that week, the man told her he had some bad news. His work was done in her city and he had to get back to his traveling. He wished her well. Jenna was angry. She was just learning what it was like to have a real friend, and now he was going to leave her. She'd go back to being hungry and waiting to find her mom dead.

"What if I went with you?"

"I'd love for you to go with me, honey, but won't your mom miss you?"

"She probably won't even know I'm gone. I could just travel with you."

"What's it going to look like a 50-year-old man hanging out with a 13-year-old girl?"

"I'll call you Daddy. People will never know." Jenna felt like she had all the answers. She was willing to do whatever it took to be around someone who genuinely cared for her. She'd never have to be hungry again.

"Oh. I don't know...," The man stood thinking.

"Please say yes. We can go right now." Jenna leapt from the park bench and wrapped her arms around him. "I'm not letting you go until you say yes."

"Well... I guess so."

After that, it was just her and the old man. They'd go from city to city and state, to state living in hotels and cars. Anything to get by. To Jenna, it felt like an adventure. She had never even been out of her own city before.

After a few weeks, he told her they were running out of money. He said that he didn't know what they could do. Suddenly, he had a great idea.

"What if you could do a few favors for a few guys, and they'd just pay us for those favors. I could find the guys and, make sure they don't hurt you so you'd be perfectly safe. It would take only a few minutes and you'd be done. We'd finally be able to get another decent meal."

Jenna hated the idea. It reminded her of the things she had to do for her mom's friends. Before she knew it, her head was shaking uncontrollably. She really didn't want to. All she could think about were bad things.

WHAM! Her dad slapped her so hard that she came back to her senses. She grabbed her face and started crying.

"I'm sorry, honey. I didn't mean to do that. I just…" He began to sob himself. They both leaned against the hood of his car, behind the dumpster. "I knew I shouldn't have let you come along with me. I just can't take care of you. I don't like having to fish inside of dumpsters to find food…" He continued to cry. "Maybe I should just take you back home. That way, you don't have to deal with this. You deserve better."

The thought of returning home stopped Jenna's tears. One hour with her dad was more fun than the entire thirteen years she had spent with her mom. "You said it would only last a few minutes?" she whimpered.

Her dad turned to face her. "Yes, honey. And, I'll make sure the guys don't do anything to hurt you."

It turned out that it lasted more than a few minutes, and it wasn't just a couple of guys. Jenna hated it, but every time she'd tell her dad, they'd get into this huge fight that ended with her face all bloody. Then, they'd lose customers for a few days because no one wanted to do anything with a chick who had a bruised face.

A few years later, they came across a customer who called himself Bobby. Jenna never believed anyone's real names because she and her dad changed theirs every few months. When her dad brought Bobby behind the building to meet with Jenna, the man stopped.

"Ay, what's with this 12-year old? I said a young woman, not a child."

"She's not 12, she's 17," her dad said. "She's of legal age."

Jenna was used to people thinking she was younger, but she didn't think she looked 12. She was actually 16 at the time, but she stopped worrying about the years. In her profession, she quickly learned that she could be whoever she wanted to be. To every customer, she gave a new story.

"Naw. I'm not interested." Bobby began to walk away.

Her dad walked with Bobby back to his car, trying to convince him to come back. Jenna patiently waited on them to return. She didn't care if they returned or not. A new customer would be right behind him anyway.

Twenty minutes later, her dad returned excited. "Honey, I got great news!" Jenna had never seen him so happy.

His excitement was contagious. She smiled too. "What is it Daddy?"

"I got to talking to Bobby. Telling him our story and all, and he has a great job for us. We'll be making more money than we have ever dreamed, and you may not have to do favors anymore."

Jenna had heard his lies many times, but his excitement was contagious.

"How's that Daddy?"

They joined Bobby's organization immediately. The job was perfect for Jenna, and she was improving every year. The organization was so intricate that it didn't even have a name, and they almost never dealt with the same people twice. All they knew was they'd get sent to a city, were given orders of what type of person they needed, then they'd deliver. The jobs could pay five to ten thousand dollars on the spot. That's how she ended up with Kayla.

The orders were to deliver a pretty teenage girl to a brothel in Edon. She and her dad loved brothel jobs because they paid the most. Brothels made thousands of dollars a day, and their girls worked for years. They were known to pay top dollar for high quality. They were told the Edon job would pay $10,000. Jenna knew the higher quality, the better pay. After Jenna proved that Kayla was worth more, they ended up getting $20,000 for her.

Her dad found a house they could rent in the nearby town of Garvey. All he had to do was pay three months cash up front. With their personal belongings in a trash bag, a folding table with two chairs, and a blow-up mattress, they camped out there as he enrolled Jenna in the nearby school. Kayla spotted Jenna on the first day.

"Hi. Are you new here?" Kayla sat at the lunch table, next to Jenna.

"Yea," Jenna looked over to examine Kayla. Pretending to be shy, she said softly, "Today is my first day." Kayla was beautiful. She had a huge smile, flawless face, perfect body and above all, she was a bouncy cheerleader. Jenna believed men loved cheerleaders.

"Oh, great. I love to show new students around."

"Okay," Jenna sputtered. She didn't know if Kayla was serious or not, but she had a mission and the sooner she completed it, the better.

"Here, I gotta get to class, but text me." Kayla scribbled her number on a piece of paper to give to Jenna before leaving the lunchroom.

Jenna texted Kayla as soon as school was over. She'd considered herself a pro after the 11 years of identifying victims and learned to follow their lead.

> *Hey. This is Jenna. The new girl. Sorry if I seemed weird earlier. I'm really shy.*

> *Aw. No reason to be shy. Why don't you come to cheer practice? You can meet my friends.*

> *I'm not the most spirited person. Could I just hang out with you after? I'd like to know what there is to do in this city.*

> *Np. I'll call you after practice.*

Jenna met up with Kayla at a nearby burger joint. Demetrius tagged along. After seeing how ditzy Demetrius was, Jenna knew that she'd be an easy target, but Jenna didn't go for easy; she went for money. Demetrius was a bulky girl, and she was a bit goofy. She seemed to also suffer from adolescent acne. But Kayla was flawless. With a look like Kayla's, Jenna was sure that she could get top dollar.

Jenna pretended to be shy and interested in Garvey and the girl's lives. She told them her mother sent her to live with her dad because she was having trouble in school. Lying was Jenna's favorite part of the job. She half believed the stories she told and fed off the interest the girls gave her. Kayla wanted to take a picture of the girls before they decided to leave.

"Come on. Let's get a quick pic before we leave."

Jenna pulled her hoodie back over her head. "No. I really don't like taking pictures."

"But you have to. I'm going to post it to the 'gram."

"You girls go head. I'm not as pretty as you. I don't want to."

"Jenna. You have to let me give you a makeover." Kayla and Demetrius smiled into her phone for a quick photo. "I promise once I'm done with you, you'll jump in front of the camera." Kayla's face was buried into her phone as she typed away. Demetrius just sat next to her, smiling while watching Kayla type.

"What are you doing with the photo?"

Kayla finished typing and put her phone away. "I have to post it to the 'gram. My followers expect an update from me several times a day."

Jenna had no idea what she was talking about, but ten minutes later, she knew it all. She used Kayla's phone to look at her page and learned everything she needed to start her research later.

Once home, she sat in front of the computer, reading everything about Kayla's history and Tubman High. She knew all about Brian, Tiffany, and Kayla's weekly schedule. Jenna needed to be in on the action. She made a fake profile picture from a photo she took from a Google search. The photo was of a body-built chic with long hair leaning over a bike. She made her profile name, Biker Girl. Jenna made sure to follow as many lame students as she could find from the high schools. It proved to be an easy, yet daunting task. She didn't finish until after midnight.

"Honey," her dad called to her, "How much longer will we be here?"

"It's going to take at least a couple of weeks."

"I don't want to be here that long."

"Daddy, we have plenty of time. You paid for three months."

"The longer we're here, the more suspicious people will become."

Her dad was really getting on her nerves. She was starting to wonder how much longer she needed him along. Her love for him had diminished. She was the brains of the whole operation. All he did was call in reinforcements as needed. The more she thought about it, she could hire people out on her own.

"This is going to be a good one Daddy. Just give me a little time. I promise, it will be worth the wait." Jenna knew that if more than 20,000 people liked Kayla, she had to be worth real money.

It only took Jenna a few tries to devise the perfect plan. She knew that for a girl as popular as Kayla, she'd have to disappear by her own free will. Otherwise, too many people would go looking for her. At first, she wanted to find some attractive guy to sweep her off her feet. Someone that Kayla would run away with. That plan didn't work. Kayla was head over heels in love with Brian.

Next, Jenna tried to speculate that a relationship was brewing between Kayla's best friend, Tiffany, and Brian, but that didn't work. Kayla was too trusting. Jenna was pissed. Something needed to work and no one could suspect Jenna of being a part of it.

Her dad was growing impatient by the day. He confronted her one day she came in from school. "Honey. You're spending all of our money on drugs and you have yet to deliver a girl."

Jenna walked past him to put her backpack down in the living room area. "I told you I just need time. The drugs help me-"

WHAM!

Before Jenna knew it, her dad was right behind her and had landed two punches on each side of her head. He caught her off guard. She fell over onto the backpack.

She covered her face with her hands, trying the block the following blows.

"What's this for? I'm working as hard as I can!" she yelled between the punches.

It didn't take long before her dad was out of breath. It was something she loved about his old age. He couldn't beat her as long as he used to.

Of all the years that they had been together, she'd only hit him back once, and one time was all she needed. He pulled a gun out on her - a gun she didn't even realize that he had. He rested the gun at her temple.

"If you ever hit me again, it will be your last day on earth." She got the picture. She was afraid to move, and he held the gun there in silence long enough for her to think that he'd really pull the trigger. She never forgot that day, and she knew he had never forgotten either.

When the torture finally ended, he left her on the floor covering herself in the fetal position. She looked up to find him seated at their folded table and chair set.

"I'm just frustrated is all," he said barely above a whisper.

She slowly walked close to him, careful not to get within arm's reach. "I know, Daddy. I promise, I'll make you proud."

She left the house and texted Kayla. Her face looked like shit and she knew she wouldn't be able to attend school the next day.

Now would be a good time to get that makeover.

Sure. You want to come by?

Yes. Please send me your address.

Jenna found Kayla's house and canvassed her neighborhood. She saw that there was access to her house in the back. She knew Kayla lived with her parents and brother, but she didn't want to be seen. She stood in the back alley and texted Kayla.

Can you meet me in your backyard? I really don't want anyone to see me like this.

Kayla was in the backyard within minutes.

"What's going on?" She gasped when she got close enough to see Jenna's face. "Who did this to you?"

"My dad did. I..." she paused for effect. She learned that from watching acting videos on YouTube. "I made him angry again. I just don't want to go to school looking like this."

"We have to go tell someone." Kayla turned to run back into her house.

Jenna grabbed her arm to stop her. "Please, Kayla. I don't want anyone else to know. I'm going to figure it all out. Just not right now. Can't you just fix my face up and make it pretty like yours?" By the time Jenna left Kayla's backyard, she was looking like a movie star.

Jenna should have known that this would be the trick. She felt dumb that she hadn't figured it out sooner. Kayla was always looking to save someone. She wanted to be a great friend to the friendless. All Jenna needed to do was be a damsel in distress. She'd play the victim card enough to get Kayla to put her guard down. It was ingenious.

Kayla was responsive to Jenna's every call. She was willing to meet her whenever she wanted to meet. She was willing to keep her dirty little secret. Kayla even started telling her own secrets to Jenna, so they'd be even. It was perfect. Jenna knew that Kayla didn't have a flawless life after all. She learned enough to know about her insecurities with pleasing her boyfriend. With not feeling loved enough by her dad. With how hard it was for her to pretend to be happy all the time. Jenna learned all the information she could so that she could use it all against her.

She had her dad bring in a reinforcement from Edon, a homeless looking guy named Jay. He wasn't the sharpest tool in the shed but turning coal into a diamond became another specialty of hers. She had Jay secure a pair of knock off shoes that looked like the shoes that Kayla would post on her Instagram page. She had planned to use the shoes to lure Kayla in some way.

Even though she knew she'd have to dodge endless videos and selfies at Kayla's birthday party, she decided to go incognito. Her cover was that she wanted to floss for her girl. Jenna wore enough makeup to render her unrecognizable. Her long gold pointy earrings were hidden underneath her long black wig. A black jacket covered her metallic shirt and she wore a black miniskirt to make sure all eyes would be drawn down her legs to her shoes. It was a hit. Everyone was gawking, especially the birthday girl.

"Oh my God, Jenna. I can't believe you have those shoes. We have to take a pic."

Jenna knew that Kayla wouldn't take no for an answer. She almost cursed herself for drawing that much attention to herself. Surely, her dad would kill her if she messed this up.

"Okay, but just one." Jenna made sure to throw her head back right when the camera flashed. She hoped that the wig and the makeup were enough to not prove that she was there.

"Really, Jenna. Where did you get those?"

"I know a guy." Jenna smiled, pretending to be coy.

Tiffany overheard their conversation. She got close enough to Jenna's ear so that only she could hear. "She thinks those are cute now but wait until she sees that her real friends got her the real thing."

Jenna pretended that she didn't hear Tiffany and walked to the kitchen to get herself a drink. She knew Tiffany didn't like her because she was starting rumors about her and Brian. That wasn't what bothered Jenna. She needed to know what Tiffany meant about the real thing. She made sure to stay within earshot of Tiffany to eavesdrop on everything she had to say.

"It's almost time for giiiifts," Tiffany sang. "We got you something special, Kayla, just wait." Jenna heard Tiffany tell Kayla right before walking into the kitchen. "Has anyone seen Brian?" Tiffany asked.

A lightbulb went off in Jenna's head. This was her only chance. She kept drugs on her for special occasions like this.

"I think I saw him go into that room back there." Jenna pointed at a room that she had seen Brian go into several times that evening. She knew that he had really gone outside to help the guys bring in more cases of beer.

"Oh, perfect," Tiffany said more to herself, "That's where we hid the shoes."

Tiffany walked to the room with Jenna sneaking quietly behind her. As soon as Tiffany opened the door, Jenna walked inside.

"What are you doing? Brian's not even in here."

"Uhm, I'm sorry. I saw him come in here earlier." Jenna looked around the room and noticed a bag on Brian's bed. "Oh, is that the gift," she pointed. "Can I see it?"

Tiffany looked annoyed, but walked over to the bed to open the bag. Jenna closed the bedroom door behind her and took off one of her earrings. While Tiffany was removing the box from the bag, Jenna pulled the ketamine filled syringe out of her jacket pocket. Tiffany began to lift the top off the brown box when Jenna drove the syringe into her butt. Tiffany jumped. Jenna had the syringe empty and behind her back by the time Tiffany turned around.

"Ouch! What the hell was that, Jenna?"

Jenna showed her the earring in her hand. "Sorry, I guess I got a little close."

By the time Tiffany stopped showing off the shoes and returned them to the bag, her speech started to slur. Jenna guided her to the bed. Tiffany's body laid limp as she moved in and out of a dream state.

Jenna moved quickly to put her evidence back into her pocket, moved the bag to the side, and removed Tiffany's clothes. She carefully placed them on Brian's desk before slipping out of the room.

She picked up a drink and rejoined the party like nothing had happened. Jenna had enough ketamine in the syringe to knock Tiffany out for hours. She knew she wouldn't remember a thing about what happened whenever she came to.

She found Kayla on the dancefloor. "What's happening, birthday girl?"

"Where have you been? I've been looking all over for you, Tiffany, and Brian."

"I was in the kitchen getting a drink. I haven't seen Tiffany or Brian." She looked around the house to pretend that she was looking for them. She noticed White Boy Steve talking to the DJ. The DJ was pointing towards her and Kayla. White Boy Steve looked nervous. She pretended not to notice, but the last thing she needed was any extra attention. She needed to get Kayla out of town quick.

Jenna noticed that Brian walked back inside. Her eyes followed him from the kitchen to his bedroom. "Look, there's Brian right there." She grabbed Kayla's hand without waiting for her response. She pulled her arm while making a bee-line to Brian's room. She opened the door to see exactly what she had planned to see. Brian in a compromising position.

Her and Kayla rushed out to the raggedy gray Honda that Jay had stolen for her to use. It came equipped with temporary tags. As Kayla cried on the way to her house, Jenna promised that she'd help her feel better.

"I'm sorry that happened, Kayla. I never thought something like that would happen."

"I should have believed you all along. I can't believe I was so naïve."

"I really did think that if you had sex with him, he would stop flirting with her. I guess I was wrong." Jenna pretended that her sexual persistence to Kayla was innocence, remembering the vial of coke she wasted trying to convince Kayla to try it.

"I should have never done it. I didn't even want to. I just wanted to make him happy, like you said. I didn't know what to do. I tried to act mature like you told me, but I'm sure I didn't do anything right. He looked at me with pity. That's probably why he did it?"

"Forget Brian. I know something that might cheer you up."

"Nothing can cheer me up, Jenna. Are you serious?"

"The real reason I wore these shoes tonight was to see if you liked them. I have a friend who can get them really cheap. I just thought-"

"Oh my God, yes! I would love to. When can we get them?"

Jenna could tell that the mention of Kayla's shoe porn was the perfect distraction she needed. "I'll call him tonight. I bet he can have them for you by morning."

Jenna tried her best to look like the perfect friend. She consoled Kayla and promised her that everything would be alright. She reminded her that she could have any guy she wanted. She told her she didn't need friends like Tiffany. She had her and Demetrius, and they would still be best friends. Although black lines drained from Kayla's red eyes, she nodded in agreement as she left the beat-up Honda to slowly walk into her house.

Jenna convinced herself that she had won Kayla over. She just needed to put the finishing touches on making her disappear.

They needed to make it seem like everything around Kayla was normal so that no one would suspect anything. She told Jay to get a car just like Brian's; unfortunately, that was the only part that Jay got right.

Jay met Kayla and Jenna at the corner store on Sunday. Jenna was supposed to introduce Jay to her so that she'd get comfortable being around him. He showed Kayla the shoes and she tried them on. She was so excited to see them on her feet that she gave Jay a hug. Jenna figured that must've been what confused him.

She noticed White Boy Steve coming out of the corner store and remembered that she was running low on her supply.

"I'll be right back," she told Jay and Kayla.

Jenna caught up with White Boy Steve before he made it to his convertible.

"Hey! What's up!"

"Hey, Jenna. You were looking hot at the party Saturday night."

"What was up with you and the DJ pointing at me? Are you telling folks my business?"

"You know I'd never do that. I don't even know you," he smirked. "You want the usual?"

"Sure. I'm trying to lift my girl's spirits." Jenna knew she had to paint Kayla as a bad girl. It would help confuse people when she disappeared. Teenagers couldn't hold water.

"Oh yea? She's trying these too?"

Jenna smiled. "Me and my girl trying to get lit."

"Well, y'all have fun then."

Kayla walked up to Jenna. "What's this about a party? I gotta get home." Stunned, Jenna stuffed her pockets while turning to eye Kayla.

"What?" Jenna knew she shouldn't have left him alone with her. "Let me see what he's talking about."

Jenna ran over to Jay. "What are you telling this girl?"

"I thought we were taking her tonight."

"No, you idiot. Did you see that guy I was talking to over there? He goes to her school."

"Let's just drop her off at home. I'll tell you the rest afterward." It was the fourth time she'd had a disagreement with Jay. On one hand, it was good that he was dumb but on the other, it was the worst thing in the world. He didn't know anything about a covert operation. She blamed her dad. He had no clue how to hire good talent.

Jenna watched as Kayla came back to the car.

"We'll drop you off." Jenna let Kayla sit in the front seat while she sunk into her seat in the back. It was perfectly fine for people to see Jay; they just didn't need to see her with Jay. Jay didn't know enough about her or her dad to point a finger at them. As long as he picked up and delivered Kayla as needed, she'd collect and be in the clear.

Jenna searched on her phone until she found a new pair of Louboutin shoes. "Have you seen these?" She handed the phone to Kayla in the front seat.

"You know I have. I just haven't been by to try them on yet."

"Jay was just telling me that a new shipment is coming in tomorrow. He can get these for you too, but you'd have to be there when the shipment comes in."

"Wait? Are you stealing these?" Kayla asked, like stealing was beneath her.

"Naw," Jay chimed in. "My cousin works at the local warehouse. He gets a crazy discount and he owes me a favor." It was the smartest thing Jenna had ever heard him say. She saw how it could work.

Kayla gave her the phone back. "But, didn't he say there was only a limited amount the employees could get? Once they're gone, they're gone," Jenna added.

"No, I have got to have these shoes. Jay you have to get them first."

"Are you sure? You'd have to come with me."

"When?"

"Tomorrow," Jenna added. "Jay, why don't you just text me when. Kayla, I'll let you know."

They dropped Kayla off. Jenna was excited envisioning how her plan worked. "Don't mess this up, Jay."

They planned that Jay would be waiting near the school until Jenna told him to come. Jay would take her to a secluded warehouse, where a few men would be waiting to drug and take her away. As soon as Kayla went in the bathroom crying about Brian, Jenna sent her the urgent text.

Sorry. I meant to tell you that Jay was on his way. The shoes are in. He's been in the back of the school waiting. He's probably left by now.

Jenna went into an empty classroom near the back of the school to spy out the window. Five minutes later, Kayla jumped into the car with Jay. By the end of the school day, Kayla had been drugged and chained inside of her new home inside the brothel. Jenna and her dad collected their money by the end of the week.

Jenna's dad pulled into the daycare parking lot. "How long ya' going to be in there?"

"The interview shouldn't take long. Just pull over to the side."

Jenna's new assignment was to make arrangements for a three-year old boy and four-year old girl. Daycares were the best place to find children because the options were great, and she could learn parenting habits before coming up with her plan. At the rate she was going, she'd retire a millionaire.

She opened the door to the Candyland themed daycare center. The receptionist greeted her with friendly eyes and a warm smile.

"How may I help you?"

"Good morning. My name is Elizabeth. I'm here for an interview."

What did you think? See what others thought and add your comments in our virtual library at www.cjkpublishing.com/library

Don't stop there. CJK Publishing has engaging stories for the entire family.

Demarcus Jones and the Solar Calendar intertwines historical facts with current events. The book series helps youth understand the plight of the African Diaspora through the adventures of a pre-teen. Reading level: ages 9 – 12. Available in print, e-book and audio-book formats.

Innovative Inner G's is a variety book that celebrates Black excellence. The coloring pages, lists, games, mazes and more are fun for the entire family. Appropriate for all ages.

When tragedy occurs, everyone claims to know what happened, but there's only one truth. Each book in the 20 People's Lies Book series begins with the facts of the disaster, with multiple witnesses to follow. Do you think you can uncover the truth before time runs out? Appropriate for ages 14+

Our subscribers are a part of every new release. Join us by visiting www.cjkpublishing.com/subscribe

www.ingramcontent.com/pod-product-compliance
Lightning Source LLC
Chambersburg PA
CBHW032004170626
46807CB00006B/2635